LOVING HIS REPORTER GIRL

A SAGE CREEK SMALL TOWN ROMANCE

BRITNEY M. MILLS

CRYSTAL CANYON PUBLISHING

CHAPTER 1

$\mathcal{L}$iam Pearson watched the sunrise from the front porch, breathing in the fall morning air. After a long day at the hospital in Grand Junction, Colorado, the day before, it was nice to sit on something other than hard waiting room chairs, especially after trying to keep Cari occupied as her mother went in for surgery.

He'd had to fight his six-year-old niece to get in the car to go home late that night. An image of her defiance played in his mind, and he smiled, realizing she was the spitting image of her mother when she did that. Cari had been lying on the hospital bed next to her mother, playing a game on his tablet. He understood somewhat the fear the young girl harbored. She'd gone through so much in her young life, and the hospital was a place of unknowns. Would her mother come back home alive after her treatments? Because her father hadn't after his car accident.

At this hour, he should be waking her up to get ready for school, but he needed the silence, the quiet reflection this moment gave him. He'd never had moments like these in

New York, and he wondered how he'd made it five years there without slowing down even a bit.

Every day over the past six months, his decision to leave investment banking and move in with his sister and niece in Sage Creek, Colorado, proved to be a good move, and better health was only the tip of the iceberg. Had someone told him he'd now own an independent bookstore, he'd have thought they'd lost a few brain cells.

Most of the stress he felt now was in regard to his sister's health. She'd been diagnosed with leiomyosarcoma the month before, after several months of fatigue, nausea, and weight loss. As stubborn as Kara Plumfield was, it had taken her fainting and blacking out on two separate occasions to convince her she needed to get checked out. But Liam hadn't imagined the whirlwind that would come of it.

They'd had to wait for the specialist to come over from Denver. The surgery from the day before had been to remove the tumor in her stomach, a procedure with several risks. But Kara had never wavered, knowing she had to do whatever she could to prolong time with her daughter.

On the doctor's recommendation, Kara had chosen to do a session of radiation before they sewed her back up. Liam just hoped it would get all of the cancerous cells and help his sister get back to her normal vivacious personality. She still gave off as much enthusiasm as she could from her hospital bed, but that spark of excitement seemed to wane each time she saw the doctor.

The door opened, and Cari walked out, her hair sticking out in every direction. She rubbed her eyes beneath her glasses and climbed into his lap, snuggling her head against his chest. For the moment, all was right with the world, and he could have stayed like that for days. He'd checked his phone several times in the half-hour since he'd been awake, knowing this morning's updates would bring critical information about his sister's health.

"How'd you sleep?" he whispered into Cari's ear.

"Okay. I had one bad dream that woke me up. But I closed my eyes and went back to sleep."

Liam smiled, kissing the top of her head. He could only imagine what she would dream about. Most likely hospitals and needles as she'd seen the nurses poke and prod her mother for blood samples over the past few weeks.

"How about pancakes for breakfast? I'll get making them while you get ready for school. How does that sound?" He leaned back and smiled as her head popped up, eyes wide.

"Can we call my mom?" Her eyelashes fluttered, and as much as Liam wanted to call his sister, he knew she still needed the rest.

He shook his head. "Your mommy's probably really tired still from the surgery yesterday. When I hear back from the hospital, we'll know we can call her. Maybe after school. Is that okay?" He watched as the sadness on her face disappeared with his proposal.

"Can I wear my purple dress?" Cari asked, bouncing up and down on his knee.

Liam turned his lips to the side and tapped his cheek with one finger, watching as she waited in suspense. "It looks like it will be a nice day. I think your purple dress would be fine."

She slid off his lap and danced on her toes in celebration before running inside. Her footsteps pounded up the stairs, the sound echoing through the hallway and out the front door.

Liam looked out at the line of trees over the tops of the houses across the street and smiled. She definitely got her zest for life from her mother.

Walking in, Liam pulled out the bag of pancake mix and measured it out, not needing to look at the directions anymore after the many times he'd made them over the past few months. He looked around the kitchen, seeing his sister's touch everywhere. Her favorite color was plum, and some of the appliances she owned were either completely that color or they had some part in that shade.

A minute or two later, Cari ran down the stairs and took up her usual seat at the table. Liam studied her face as she stared at the griddle, her eyes wide with excitement. He'd never met anyone who loved pancakes more than his niece.

He tried to hide a smile as his eyes traveled to her hair. It looked as though she'd tried to put it into a ponytail, but with the large bumps on top and several sections sticking out on the sides, she looked like she'd been in a tussle rather than just waking up.

"Here are a few hot off the griddle," he said with a smile, piling two pancakes on a paper plate. He poured syrup over the top of it and gave her a fork. "When you're done, we'll have to do something with your hair."

Cari turned to him with a scowl. "I already did it."

"I just want to fix one little part," Liam said, making a small space in between his forefinger and thumb.

Cari liked being independent, especially with her clothes and hair. Liam wasn't all that good at the fancy hair Kara could create with a few elastic bands, but he'd learned fast how to braid and use bows to his advantage.

"Fine. But we get to go to the park after school today if I let you." She held out her fork, using it to emphasize each word. Her negotiation skills were something to admire.

Liam chuckled, the serious face of his niece reminding him so much of Kara when they were younger. She was three years older than him and should have the world ahead of her. He just hoped the results of the surgery would be favorable and they could get back to their lives.

Twenty minutes later, they were out the door and walking the few blocks to Sage Creek elementary school.

"Don't forget. We're going to the park after school," Cari said, her lips pursed and her chin raised.

"If it doesn't rain, we will."

She folded her arms against her chest. "You said we could go to the park. I think we should go even in the rain."

Raising both hands in surrender, Liam chuckled. "We'll see what we can do."

Cari hesitated, and Liam could tell the wheels were turning from his statement. "If we don't go to the park, then you owe me a big bowl of ice cream."

"Deal." Liam pulled her into a hug, but she tore away and waved, disappearing into the crowd of children playing on the playground. Liam smiled, remembering when he'd do that with his own mother.

His thoughts turned to his mother as he walked back to the bookstore on Main Street. It was just south of the coffee shop, probably the best spot they could have hoped for as people would grab their beverage and walk over, looking for their latest read. It had been their mother's dream to own one, as she loved reading or anything that had to do with books. In his mind's eye, Liam could see her chatting away when he was as young as Cari, talking about how the characters in the book she was currently reading "moved" her.

It had been Kara's idea to open the store in Sage Creek, and while Liam had been skeptical that a bookstore would survive in a small town like this, he'd put up the money to get it started and trusted his sister that it would all work out. Five months in, every day he was surprised by how much income they were making and the number of people he spoke to about this book or that.

Now, New York seemed light-years away, as if that had been a long dream he'd had and this was what his reality looked like. He was content for the most part, aside from worrying about his sister. But he wouldn't have been able to help out like this, taking care of Cari and driving back and forth to Grand Junction for this appointment or that surgery, if he still lived across the country.

Opening the door to the bookstore, Liam flipped the lights on and walked to set his current book down on the counter. It was a mystery, one that many of the citizens of the town had already bought or borrowed. MK Malone was the hot topic for many, and Liam was pleasantly surprised when he'd finally broken down and started reading it.

He'd always thought cozy mysteries were for girls, as the main character was usually some snoopy woman who couldn't mind her own business. But the way the author had crafted the characters and the plot so far, Liam had to smile several times throughout the first half as he realized the author had linked with points A, B, and C from the beginning of the book. Such nuances he'd overlooked until they'd begun to come into play. He found himself looking forward to seeing how it ended.

He walked in the direction of the small breakroom in back, past the rows of shelves and the small study desks along the wall, to place his leftovers in the fridge for lunch before he moved to the large event room. He'd ordered several new computers to go next to the row of desks, and with all the little trinkets he'd started stocking, he'd drawn in more and more customers.

When looking for a place to open up shop, Kara had the idea to find something big enough for the books and space large enough to allow people to talk about them. After looking throughout Sage Creek and finding nothing suitable at first, Liam asked the landlord if they could rent two units and place a few doors in the wall that divided them to allow passage between the two. He'd approved without hesitation, glad to rent out both.

The bell over the door chimed, and Liam walked back to the counter to see who it was. "Oh, hey, Tanner." He walked over and shook the hand of the owner of the hardware store. They'd hung out quite a bit before his sister had taken a turn for the worse, but with the extra appointments and surgery, it had been a while since they'd gotten together. "What can I do for you today?"

"I'm just wondering if you have any books on sewing?"

Liam raised his eyebrow, curious as to why Tanner Hart would suddenly need something for sewing. He'd been the quarterback for his high school and had even gone to school on scholarship. Liam knew a lot of guys who could sew, but that was something he couldn't picture Tanner doing. "Yeah, here in the Arts and Crafts section."

They walked over to one of the back rows, and Liam waved across the selection that spanned several shelves.

Tanner's eyes went wide, and he frowned. "It's for my mother, so any advice you have would be great. She wanted one with embroidery. Is that when they make a whole bunch of x's on the white fabric?"

Liam laughed and slapped Tanner on the back. "Yep. Okay, here at the bottom, we have a lot of those kinds of books, different themes along here. If there isn't something you think she'd like, I can order one for you. When do you need it by?"

"Tomorrow," Tanner said, a sheepish grin on his face. He bent down and looked over the books displayed there, pulling out one with fairytale designs. "I'm going to go with this one. If she doesn't like it, I'll send her here and you can order her something."

Liam turned and walked back to the counter, realizing he

hadn't started the computer up just yet. "At least you thought about her the day before her birthday, right?"

"Yep." Tanner chuckled and pulled out his wallet, extending a credit card toward Liam. "What are you doing in a couple of weeks? A bunch of us were going to head up into the mountains on side-by-sides the weekend after Colton gets back from his honeymoon, and we haven't seen you in a while. You should come."

Focusing on the computer, Liam nodded, swiping the card through the reader. "It sounds like a lot of fun, but I've got Cari."

"No news yet about Kara?" Tanner's lips drooped, making him look ten years older. He was one of a handful of people in town who truly knew what was going on with Liam's sister. It was hard enough having his sister in the hospital, but in a town like this, Liam would get attacked by the questions and pity stares.

Aside from Tanner, Colton Maxfield, the builder of a new subdivision and one of the first people to welcome him in town, along with his fiancée, Becca, and two or three of the older ladies in town were about the only people who knew her condition. Becca owned the flower shop up Main Street, and the one time Liam had broken down and told Colton just after Kara's diagnosis, she'd sent several bouquets to the hospital.

"I've just been waiting for a call that Kara has woken up. And any news on her counts. It might be too early to know too much, but I'll take whatever information they'll give me. I'm hoping she can come home next week, but who knows."

Tanner signed his name on the touchscreen and replaced the pen. "What if I arrange for someone to watch Cari? Since it's fall, we won't have light for too long."

The idea was tempting, but Liam wasn't going to hold his breath. Tanner was a good-looking single guy. There wasn't a chance he'd actually remember to talk to someone about babysitting Tanner's niece once he walked out the door. At least, that would have been Liam's mentality just a few years ago.

"I mean, if you can find someone, then I'll see what I can do. It all depends on when Kara gets out and what she needs right now."

Tanner smiled. "Awesome. I'll get it all set up." He waved goodbye as he headed out with the book in hand.

Liam grinned, thinking of the fun it would be to adventure into the hills behind Sage Creek, something not possible in Manhattan. But then he remembered his sister and niece and brought himself back to reality. There was no way he was going to let either one of them down now, when they needed him most. He'd already done that to his sister once, and he wasn't about to repeat it.

Checking the time, he moved into action, knowing the weekly book club would be arriving in a couple of hours. It had become a tradition for a group of over a dozen ladies to stop in once a week to talk about the books they were reading. It was great for business and even for a good chuckle when Liam managed to catch snippets of the conversation.

When the seats were all arranged in the large room they used for bigger gatherings, Liam settled behind the counter. He settled in with the MK Malone book, intrigued as the clues came in for who had killed the town chef.

Things were quiet for the next two hours, and as he finished the last page, it felt like he'd just stepped out of a new world and into his regular one. A thought somewhat depressing.

He looked at the back cover, reading about the author, but the biography was only two sentences long and no picture.

The thought crossed his mind that he should contact the

author to do a reading and sign some books in the next month. They'd had two other authors visit since the store opened, which always helped sales go up as people flooded into the store. The book club wasn't the only group of people reading the cozy mysteries, and he couldn't keep the books in stock. That could be a big enough pull to draw the author into their sleepy little town.

The bell rang on the other side of the wall, and Liam jotted on a sticky note to find contact info on the author when he finished helping the book group settle in.

"Ah, Liam, dear. It's so good to see you again. How is your sister?" Mrs. McCready asked. She was a small woman, her hair looking like a snowfall around her shoulders. Reaching up, she patted his cheek as though he were still a small child. She reminded him of the grandparents he'd never met, having lost them when he was much younger than Cari.

Liam gave her a small smile. "I'm just waiting to hear how things turned out with the tests." He waved his cell phone as if it would summon the call from the hospital right then.

Mrs. McCready gasped. "I hope it was all clear. That would be such a wonderful miracle. Gordon has some more tests on Tuesday, so we'll be heading to Grand Junction then. Do let me know if I can bring Kara anything, will you?"

The McCreadys had found out about Kara's condition by accident, as Mr. McCready was taken in after some abnormalities in his bloodwork. Liam and Kara had just walked out of the doctor's office located in the hospital after getting the news of her condition, and the McCreadys had been there. In a way, it was comforting to share the burden with a couple who'd already felt like family since he'd moved to Sage Creek.

"Yes, ma'am." Liam moved to pick up a piece of paper on the floor. "Is there anything else I can get for you before your party arrives?"

"I don't think so, dear. Thank you for letting us use this room, as always. It's better than all of us trying to fit into each other's houses, I'll tell you that!"

With a smile, Liam said, "Anytime. I'll just be in the back if you need me. Today's shipment should be arriving at any moment, and I'll have a few extra copies of the book you're going to discuss."

He turned and strode away, hoping to avoid the rest of the ladies in the group as the door opened and the noise level increased. While they were all very nice, he could see them calculating ways to introduce him to the single ladies in their lives, and that wasn't something he wanted or needed right now. He was focused on taking care of his niece and keeping the bookstore running, in the hope that his sister would be back in his life, bossing him around like she always had. Relationships were sticky, and he'd learned enough from his last one to know he was better off making his own decisions.

Life was easier without the worry of losing someone he loved. He'd already done that three times, with his parents and his brother-in-law. He just hoped it wouldn't happen with Kara too.

CHAPTER 2

 anielle Holloway gripped the steering wheel to her crossover SUV, willing the rollercoaster of emotions to even out a bit. She entered the narrow pass that led to Sage Creek, grateful to be at the end of her trip, but the feeling of failure increased with every mile traveled.

She was never supposed to reside in Sage Creek for longer than a few days, not since graduation from high school at least. That had been the pact she'd made to herself the moment she left for college eight years ago. Now, with a pink slip sitting in her briefcase on the seat next to her and her name muddied by newspaper ink, it was a sign that unless a miracle occurred, she'd have to stay in her hometown much longer than that.

Her original plan was to come back that weekend to see her best friend, Becca, and Colton get married, spend her obligatory few days, and then head out, jetting off to her next assignment as a media correspondent for one of the larger news outlets in Los Angeles. But word about her presence at a local protest against the city government had been documented through pictures and a giant headline screaming her name two days ago. Even with the near begging Danielle had done Monday morning, the answer her boss gave her was that she couldn't report the news if she was the news.

She'd been up for a promotion, one that was a long time coming, which made the dismissal hurt that much more. But she'd built her career from nothing, and she could do it again if she needed to. At the moment, though, no news station or paper in California would hire her. Maybe if she found somewhere near her hometown but not actually in Sage Creek, she'd have more luck.

Tapping the brake as she rolled down Main Street, she glanced at the shops as she passed, her stomach plummeting as she thought about her bleak future. Her best friend had only been able to leave this town and the county four months ago for the first time in years, but the moment Danielle graduated, she'd done everything she could to get out, feeling claustrophobic.

The fact that Becca's wedding was only four weeks after the proposal still sent her mind into spirals, but that was because it would be a miracle if Danielle ever got married. She didn't doubt that Becca and Colton were perfect for each other.

She passed Mill Street, then Canyon, and finally turned onto Bryce Street, one of the last roads before the town hit the bottom of the mountains. Velda Gibson stood outside, watering her flowers, and Danielle waved, plastering on a fake smile as she pressed the gas down a bit more. The older woman had always kept an eye out for Becca, usually notifying Danielle when she needed to reach out to her friend from whatever hotel or resort she was staying in around the world. But today was not a day when she wanted to chance the intuition of the diner owner. She had to save all the energy she had to put on a façade in front of her mother.

The light blue house at the end of the street seemed

smaller than Danielle remembered. The last time she'd been in Sage Creek was when she came home from an assignment in Europe and drove Becca to Denver to confess her feelings for Colton, her now-fiancé and, as of this weekend, her would-be husband.

As Danielle pulled into the driveway, she focused on her breathing. Short, slow breaths would help her keep her calm for however this conversation would go.

Pulling on the handle to release the door of her car, Danielle got out and swiped at the crumbs from her cheese crackers on her black slacks. Taking a deep breath, she wondered if she should tell her mother now that she was jobless, or if it was best to wait until after the wedding. She didn't need the pity stares from the whole town and Becca worrying more about what Danielle was going to do with her life rather than focusing on her wedding.

She still held a thread of hope that one of the other agencies would call her, offering her the position of a lifetime. After winning several awards, she hadn't expected it to be so hard to find another job. But it was as if the chief editors looked at her as a menace now instead of understanding the facts about why she'd been at the protest. All anyone saw was the sign she held in her hand, telling people to talk to their leaders about chemical waste being dumped in the Santa Ana River.

It was going to take longer than a few days to empty her apartment in Anaheim, which was why she'd only packed one suitcase.

Squaring her shoulders to take in the older Victorian home she'd been raised in, Danielle let out a breath. Home again.

"You can do this," she said, walking up to the front door. "This isn't forever. You'll get another job and be off traveling the world once again." The pep talk relaxed her, helping her thoughts to line up instead of running around like children after eating candy.

Opening the old screen door, Danielle noticed the slit in the screen and the peeling paint on the frame. Her mother was usually so meticulous with those kinds of things, appearance being everything in this small town. That must have been where Danielle got her particularity.

Walking in, Danielle dropped her keys into the dish on the table in the entry. "Mom! Are you home?"

The house was quiet for several seconds before Danielle heard a creak coming from what sounded like the family room. Leaving her luggage by the door, she moved in that direction, grateful to see her mother, Mary-Kate, standing next to her favorite armchair, her signature smile aimed at her daughter.

"Dani. I didn't expect you home this early. Velda and I were taking bets that you'd show up ten minutes before the ceremony this weekend." Her mother walked forward and wrapped her arms around Danielle's waist. The smell of her soap wafted to Danielle's nose, triggering several memories of her past.

"It's good to see I can actually surprise you two." Danielle took a step back, grinning.

Her mother sat down again, and Danielle hesitated, feeling like if she got too comfortable, she'd have to spill the beans about her job.

As a media correspondent, Danielle had gone through the full range of emotions as she covered different projects around the world, from contaminated water to the state of some communities in Africa. But her mother just saw it as her running off, trying to avoid things she thought Danielle should want in her life as a twenty-seven-year-old. A home. A relationship. Roots.

Taking a seat on the couch, Danielle leaned back, feeling the familiar spring dig into her back.

"Have you been by to see Becca yet? She's come by every couple of days over the past month, just gushing about the wedding. I think she's missed planning everything with you." Her mother gave her a sad smile.

"You know how I feel about weddings, especially since the last one didn't go over very well for her. And I helped out quite a bit on that one." Danielle lifted her hand to inspect her nails, not liking the way her mother's stare unnerved her. "I had to go to Florida to cover the hurricane, Mom. I'm sure she'll be a beautiful bride no matter what decorations she's picked out this time."

Danielle shifted, hoping to rid herself of the guilt pricking her insides. She could have gotten out of that assignment, but she'd wanted to be there in the action, wanted to be able to report it to the people of Southern California. Her aspirations had always been to make it to national television, but it seemed she might not achieve that dream.

"Did you organize a bridal shower for her?" her mom asked.

Biting her bottom lip, Danielle felt panic take over. "I was supposed to do that?"

"You are the maid of honor. Since she has no family but us, we should do something, don't you think?"

"Yes. But how am I supposed to pull that off right now? If I had a week I could maybe pull something together. But a couple of days? I don't even know who to contact to come." Danielle sighed, sinking deeper into the couch. Why Becca hadn't fired her as her best friend and maid of honor long before now, she wasn't sure why.

Her mother reached over and patted her hand. "Well, you'll just have to make up for it now. Let's see...it's Tuesday. So, you've got four days before the wedding, and I've got a lot of the shower put together. I sent out invitations two weeks ago, and I have several decorations I found when I went over to Grand Junction last month. I suggest you go talk to Velda to figure out food."

"Mom, you are seriously the best. Thank you." Danielle breathed a sigh of relief. She could handle the food part. The actual execution of the event would be another story, but she'd reported in gale-force winds before. A bridal shower shouldn't be hard.

"I knew you needed a little help, so I got the list of people to invite from Colton. It will be a joint party, so the guys will be there too. And then who knows what adventure you'll be off on next?" As wide as her smile looked, Danielle noted the sadness in her mother's eyes. She had always encouraged her daughter's writing dreams, but traveling to dangerous areas of the world was out of her comfort zone. Was it because she never really had that chance?

"I was thinking of hanging out here a bit longer, if you don't mind." Looking out the corner of her eye, Danielle watched an excited expression take over the slight frown.

"Really? I would love that, Dani. It's been so quiet around here, and you haven't been here for our annual fall hike in years." There were tears in her mother's eyes, and Danielle sucked in a breath, wishing the guilt wasn't driving itself into her chest. Maybe being in Sage Creek was a blessing in disguise. Spending time with her mother always seemed to help sort things out.

The fall hike was something she and her mother started when Danielle was a young girl, months after her father had walked out and never come home. They'd wander up through the trails behind Sage Creek, taking in the beautiful colors.

"If it's so quiet, you should host a party. Then all the guys will be wanting to date you." Danielle wriggled her eyebrows and grinned as her mother squirmed at the comment.

"That's rich, coming from the girl who's anti-relationship. You know how I feel about that. I had a hard enough time putting up with your father's quirks until the day he left us. There's no way I'm going to worry about having another man to cater to in my lifetime." Her mother was fighting a grin, and Danielle wondered if her mother's long-held feelings were starting to change. She could imagine how hard it would be to live alone, which was probably why she loved the thrill of airports and hotels so much. The loneliness couldn't catch up if she didn't give it a chance.

Danielle raised her hands. "It was just a joke, Mom. If you're happy, then you shouldn't change anything."

Her mother's hand covered Danielle's on the arm of the sofa. "Are you happy, Danielle?"

"Of course." The words came out quickly, but as she let the question turn in her mind, she wondered if it was really true. Would she be happy if she never got to travel again? Report on big events?

"Then I'm happy." Her mother leaned back and pulled her watch close to her eyes. "It looks like it's time to head over for book club. Will you come? We could use a little spice."

Chuckling a bit, Danielle said, "Let me guess. Sharon Crestview will be there." The woman was around Mary-Kate's age but tried to take over just about everything she did.

Her mom nodded. "She's the one who picked out today's book. One written by an author I've never heard of before. MK Malone?" With her mom's eyes staring at her, Danielle did her best to hide her shock.

MK Malone was a name she was all too familiar with, as it was the pen name she'd chosen before releasing the three cozy mysteries she'd written. Writing had always been a passion for her, but she'd viewed it as something that couldn't support her in life, and there was no way she could use her own name while she worked for the news station.

"Hmmm. That's interesting. I don't think I've read any of those." Only like a thousand times when she'd had to edit and reedit, trying to get the plot and characters just right.

"Let's go. You'll get to see the new bookstore." Her mother stood, walking over to the table by the door where her purse sat.

Danielle stood and followed her. "Bookstore? Since when does Sage Creek have a bookstore?" She grabbed her wallet from the small suitcase she'd brought in and walked out the door behind her mother.

"It's been open a few months now. I think they opened it about a month before you came home from Europe. It's been doing really well. Run by a good family, and it's nicer than the library. I've been telling Mayor Watkins for years that the library could use an update."

"What did you think of the book, Mom?" Her curiosity got the better of her. She wasn't sure why her heart started pounding, but she focused on the sidewalk beneath her feet as they walked down the sidewalk, preparing herself for criticism. With the cool fall breeze, it was the perfect day for a walk around town.

Her mother turned, her lips pinched together as though trying to decide something. "I liked it. I don't usually do well with mysteries as I have a hard time following who the possible suspects could be, but this one did well at making it a mystery while I still followed the overall plot."

"You liked it, huh?" Danielle wasn't sure why she kept needling the conversation along, but it felt good to have her mother praise her work, even if she didn't realize it. The only people in the world who knew about the author's real identity were Danielle's editor, proofreader, and cover designer. She hadn't even chanced telling Becca.

Her mother thumbed through the pages of the book and smiled. "I really liked it. I was in suspense without nightmares later on. There were a few times I screamed out, wishing I could tell the character to run and not look under the bed." She chuckled, her cheeks red.

One of the things Danielle wished for was to be a little more like her mother. The woman was sweet and kind, always thinking of others. People always complimented her on her positive attitude, and with everything she'd gone through in her life, that was a feat.

It had been so long since Danielle had to think of anyone but herself and her career. She didn't have to stay in Sage Creek forever, but maybe she could change a few things before she headed out. A true journalist should care about the person behind the story, and for too long she'd been trying to get the latest scoop in the hopes of a promotion. She needed to be more like Mary-Kate Holloway.

"I'm sure the author would take that as a compliment, Mom." Danielle couldn't help the grin on her face. If only she had the guts to tell her that the author was her own daughter.

CHAPTER 3

*L*iam walked into the store from the back door, wheeling the last few boxes that had been delivered an hour before over to the main floor of the shop. His eye caught on a waving hand, and he turned to see what was needed.

Taking a few steps in the direction of the circle, he stopped and bent down beside Mrs. McCready as she sat in a chair by the door to the other room. "What can I do for you, ma'am?" He gave her a slight smile, hoping it would be a quick request. He could already feel the several sets of eyes boring into him, waiting to find him a girlfriend. Though he'd managed to avoid it since he arrived in town, it was getting harder to fend off their requests.

"Did you, by chance, get some extra books in today? We have a few gals who would like to purchase a copy." The woman smiled at him, and Liam had to bite his upper lip to keep from laughing as he noticed her deep purple lipstick had rubbed off onto her front teeth.

He nodded and stood back up. "I do. Let me go see which box they're in, and I'll bring a few copies."

He'd never been so grateful she'd been sitting closest to the door leading to the rest of the store, just so he could get a moment to breathe without the eyes of the town on him. Maybe it was from reading that book earlier that he was starting to get more paranoid.

The MK Malone books were at the bottom of his dolly. He removed six or seven copies, hoping it would be enough for the group. Starting with Mrs. McCready, he then asked, "Who else needs a copy of the book?" He held one up, waving it around.

"I need one," a woman said, causing Liam's attention to turn to the left. He moved into the center of the circle and took it to her.

"Just pay at the register after your meeting is finished," Liam said, giving her a polite smile.

The woman, who he thought was named Whitney, gave him a coy smile, causing Liam to take a few steps back and bump into the table filled with goodies. He was able to catch his balance before tumbling down, but adrenaline rushed through him. A familiar face smiled back at him as he looked up, and he turned, grateful she wasn't laughing at him.

"Mrs. Holloway, do you have one?" He extended one in her direction.

The woman reached over and snatched her book from the lap of the woman sitting next to her. "This one is mine. My daughter just got in last night and hasn't had a chance to read it. She's quite the bookworm, and I'm sure she'd love a copy." There was a twinkle in her eye before she turned to her daughter next to her.

Liam followed her gaze and took in a woman with light brown hair, a few strands near the front more of a honey color. Her hazel eyes were soft, and the color of her lips a bright pink. He found he'd been staring at them for longer than was comfortable and knew he needed to do something.

She was beautiful, which threw him off as he'd usually been attracted to dark-haired brunettes in the past.

Her eyes went wide as she gave her mother a pleading look, and Liam worked to mask his smile at the situation. No doubt her mother was trying to play matchmaker, just like the others in the group. She was beautiful, but he had to remember he wasn't putting himself back on the dating market.

Stretching out his hand, he asked, "Would you like one, Miss…?"

"Holloway. Danielle Holloway. I think I'll be fine without it, thanks." She moved her hand up to wave him off, and her gaze moved away from his face. Her knee started moving up and down repeatedly, and Liam moved away, wondering if she felt the same way he did about relationships.

An odd sense of disappointment flowed through him, and he nodded, stepping back and searching the group for anyone else who needed a book.

Once he'd taken care of the rest of them, he walked back into the main part of the store to cut open boxes and focus on stocking the new books. Several times, the face of the Holloway girl popped up and he'd push it away, chuckling that he would start thinking about someone he'd seen for all of fifteen seconds. He hadn't really thought about women his age in a while, but that could be because there were only a few of them in this small town.

He was on the last box over by the section of sci-fi and fantasy books when the women filtered into that part of the room. He often made a lot of money after book club meetings, and now whenever a club wanted to use his space, he was more than willing to host.

Leaving the box next to the shelf, he walked over to the register. A line had already formed behind Sharon Crestview. The woman could be overbearing, but Liam had found that if he kept the conversation polite and short, he didn't have to worry about being on her blacklist.

He came in halfway through the conversation and usually tried to keep to himself, but the conversation intrigued him.

"I'll still never forget Danielle coming out of the bathroom during the Founder's Day Festival dinner with toilet paper trailing behind—"

"I think that's quite enough, Sharon."

Liam looked up to see the muscle in Mrs. Holloway's jaw flexing, her eyes narrowed in on the woman at the front of the line.

Sharon giggled and waved her hand. "Oh, she was young."

Liam wondered what response Mrs. Holloway would give, when Danielle stepped up from behind her mother. "I seem to remember the Fourth of July celebration a few years ago when you decided to wear white pants—"

"That's enough." Sharon's face drained of color as she turned, pushing two books toward Liam. "I'll take these, please."

Focusing on ringing up the books helped Liam fight the smile pulling at the corners of his mouth. He didn't look the woman in the face until he handed her the receipt and said, "Have a nice day." With his gaze raised, he caught sight of Danielle behind two other women, her lips pursed as she watched the woman walk out the door. She definitely had spunk.

He worked through the next two customers and was surprised by the stack of books Danielle placed on the counter.

Liam glanced down to her books and asked, "All these for you?" As he looked at the titles of each of the books, he realized how many of them were cozy mysteries. A few were romance novels, but it intrigued him.

"Yep. I like to read." She shrugged and pulled out her

wallet as Liam started scanning the barcodes of the ten books in front of him.

"And then she leaves the books on all my shelves at home while she travels around the world." Mrs. Holloway tried to glare at her daughter, but the smile gave her away. Standing next to each other, the two women looked like they could be sisters more than mother and daughter. But of the little he knew from Danielle over the last hour, it seemed her personality had more spice to it compared to the sweetness of her mother.

"Cozy mysteries, I take it. What do you think of MK Malone after your discussion with the older ladies?" He focused on scanning the last barcode before he glanced up to see her reaction.

"I'm not that far in yet. But the key to a good cozy is if you can't spot the killer within the first five chapters." She gave him a mischievous smile, and Liam turned to the computer, totaling the purchase.

"I'll keep that in mind." He told her the total and waited as she searched for a card in her wallet. "Are you part of the big wedding going on this weekend? I doubt you'll finish reading all these before the weekend is over." Liam tried to make it sound casual, but from her narrowed eyes, she wasn't buying it.

"I'm extending my stay a few more weeks, but I could probably read all this in one weekend—if I didn't have other obligations, that is." She raised her honey-colored eyes to his and raised one eyebrow. "What about you? What do you like to read?"

"I can read just about anything, except the straight romance stuff. Those are a little hard to get through for me." He motioned to one of the books he'd placed in a monogrammed cloth bag for her and looked up to see Danielle's wide grin. Something about it made him wish he didn't have a line of women ready to buy books just so he could talk to her a bit more.

"I can understand that. Mysteries and thrillers are my favorite right now, but I thought I'd give a few of the quick romance reads a try."

Liam's fingers brushed hers as she handed him a card, causing warmth to rush through his hand.

He turned and swiped the card, trying not to focus on the little tingles still in his fingers. He handed her the receipt after the payment was finalized. "Thanks for shopping at Just One More Chapter." He handed the bag to her, and she nodded, stepping to the side as her mother placed several books on the counter.

Once the two of them were out the door, he looked up to find a long line waiting for him. He picked up the pace, knowing these ladies were going to give him a piece of their mind or get suspicious as to his curiosity about the woman who'd just walked out the door.

CHAPTER 4

*D*anielle was twenty pages into one of the cozy mysteries she'd purchased earlier that day, reading as she waited for Becca to show up. They'd agreed to meet up at Sage Creek Diner for a bite to eat before they went through all the finalization for the reception plans. She'd ordered fries and a shake, not sure whether there would be time to eat later.

She'd read the same paragraph several times, but she kept picturing one of the main characters with the face of the guy from the bookstore, his light blue eyes etched into her memory.

Something about him signaled that owning a bookstore wasn't his first career, but she still couldn't figure out exactly what that sign was. Whatever the mystery was, it intrigued her.

When he'd asked if she'd read her own book, her heart skipped a beat, surprised by the sincerity in his expression. With his blond hair, broad shoulders, and a love of books, the guy was checking all her boxes. But she couldn't even think about anything happening between them. She'd be gone soon enough, and life was easier if she didn't have to recover from a broken heart or her mother's dashed hopes that she might settle down in Sage Creek.

"I'm so glad you're here," Becca's voice came from behind her.

Danielle stood, stepping into the hug Becca offered. After the week she'd had, she needed some support, even if the people around her didn't understand what was going on in her life. She'd tell them when she found the right opportunity, but she had to make it through the wedding first.

They both dropped into the booth, Becca leaning over and stealing one of Danielle's fries.

"Hey! Those are mine." Danielle laughed at Becca's expression, her eyes wide and chewing slowly as if she hadn't done anything at all.

"I've been so good lately, and here you are, ordering all the grease." Becca laid a large binder on the table and placed her purse on the seat next to her. Turning back to Danielle, she asked, "How was the drive back? Hopefully, it wasn't too bad since the fall weather's been nice, right?"

"It was good. Just the usual desert and traffic." Just rehashing the failure of her life for six hours. Danielle took a fry and dipped it into the shake, taking a bite as Becca wrinkled her nose.

"I don't know why you like that. Gross." Her disgust faded quickly as a smile returned and she flipped open the binder. "Okay, so here is the itinerary for the weekend." She turned the book around and slid it in front of Danielle.

Pulling it closer, Danielle wasn't surprised at the number of activities on the list. "You really think a spa day can be done in ninety minutes? We won't even have time to make it over to the wedding ceremony if we do that in such a short amount of time."

Becca bit her bottom lip and pulled the paper back in

front of her. "You're right. What was I thinking? This is why I wish you'd come home sooner." She paused and opened her eyes wider with a tilt of her head. That was code for Becca's guilt trip. "Apparently, I can't make rational decisions by myself." She took out a pen and leaned over to write something to the side of the itinerary before glancing up at Danielle.

"Whoa, now. Wait a minute. I never said that; I was just trying to be helpful. Did someone say you couldn't make rational decisions?" Danielle reached her hand out, trying to pull the pen away from Becca's strong grip, but Becca pulled her arm back with a jerk, succeeding at holding on to the pen. Danielle gave her a fake frown, draping her arm over the itinerary so Becca couldn't make any more changes.

With a sniffle, Becca held the pen out, her eyes focused on it. "Well, no. But I can feel it. It's times like these when I miss my mother most." A tear escaped, and Danielle moved to the other side of the booth, pulling her best friend toward her. Becca leaned her head on Danielle's shoulder while Danielle did her best to channel the life of a statue, knowing her friend just needed to cry it out.

When the sniffles slowed down, Danielle said, "No one is saying you can't make decisions. Every bride in the world has to have help in deciding what to do for their wedding. I think it's the clouded vision of being in love that sometimes makes it hard to see things like I just did. Let's figure this out and get you married this weekend, okay?"

Becca sat up, wiping at the tears with both hands, and nodded. "I like it," she said, her voice thick from the tears.

Scanning the list again, Danielle sighed. "Okay, I know you want this to be a lot of fun, but we have four days until the ceremony. You've got every moment planned from now until then. Why don't we pick one thing for every night, starting on Thursday, and then just see how things go from there? You can move pedicures and hair back a few hours to give you time to look perfect for your wedding day." She grinned and winked, which allowed Becca to relax a little bit. "Then people will have time to just breathe and enjoy the experience. Besides, we're in Sage Creek. We can bowl any time we want." Danielle pointed to one of the activities, scrunching her face.

Becca laughed so hard she snorted. "When you make that face, I just—I can't help but laugh."

"And snort," Danielle added, laughing, an ache forming in her side. "I haven't been home for long, but I'm pretty sure I'm still banned from the bowling alley."

"I still can't believe you caused so much damage. It's been what, eight years, and Roger still left the patched section in the ceiling where your ball hit. The light still flickers, though."

Danielle slid back against the booth, laughing over the memory. They'd gone for a day activity before prom, and she and her date had to leave after the fourth frame.

Becca took the paper again and crossed out several things, writing for over a minute before looking up at Danielle. "I actually feel really good about this now. The gal planning my wedding had me thinking I needed to do a crazy amount of stuff to make it fun for the guests, but I guess she's not used to the small-town stuff."

"Did you get Susie Jones?" Danielle asked, dipping another fry into her ice cream.

Becca frowned, shaking her head. "No, some famous girl booked her a couple weeks before Colton proposed. I know I've always been a little annoyed with her, but she has an eye for wedding planning."

"Did you get to choose most of the things you wanted, though?"

Becca looked a bit sheepish and said, "The flowers?"

Rolling her eyes, Danielle said, "Well, duh. If you had let her hire out your flowers to someone else, I would have thought you'd been abducted. What did you want most that you don't have set up right now?"

Taking a few minutes, Becca finally said, "The venue. She wanted it to be inside the rec center, but I really want it up by the pond. You know how much I love it there. It wouldn't fit the whole town, but it would fit the people we really want to be there. And it's kind of our spot, mine and Colton's."

Stuffing a scoop of the melted shake into her mouth, Danielle typed a note to herself on her phone. After swallowing, she said, "Okay, I'll work on that. Anything else we need to do?"

Becca pulled out a stack of papers and flipped through them, marking things off here and there. After a while, she said, "I think that's good for now. That was the biggest thing. Velda was worried about the rain, but even if it rains, all we need is to say I do, and then I'm married to Colton Maxfield, man of my dreams."

The beam on her face made Danielle want to gag, but she forced a smile on her face and ate an overly large scoop of ice cream. The extreme cold caused a brain freeze, probably saying something about how she was wired, but at the moment, Danielle was just trying to get through all the mushiness of her best friend's wedding.

After Saturday, Becca would have Colton by her side for the rest of her life. Danielle had never worried about not having someone at her side, always able to do everything on her own—even travel to places like Rome, London, Egypt, and Peru. But now that she thought about it, those places would have been even better with someone to share it with.

Well, her best friend, anyway.

Pushing that aside, Danielle said, "You really love him, huh?"

"Of course. He's amazing and sweet. And he pushes me to get out of my comfort zone just enough to help me conquer things."

"Where are you going on your honeymoon?" Danielle recalled how nervous Becca had been to cross the county limits when she went after Colton earlier that year.

A hesitant smile passed over her face. "On a road trip is all Colton told me."

Danielle grinned. "That'll be so fun. I know you're probably panicking right now, but he'll be right there the whole time. Then you'll be all ready to take a cruise." She wiggled her eyebrows, hoping Becca would see she was teasing.

"I hope you're right. How are things with you? Anyone of interest I should know about?" Becca's somber expression had morphed into one of curiosity.

Danielle threw the wrapper from her straw, getting it stuck in Becca's hair. Tipping her head down, she looked up at Becca. "Did you really just ask me that?"

"Life happens. Love happens, Danielle. Look at me. There was no way I was going to marry someone after what happened to my family, and then on my previous wedding day. I was sure I had bad luck and would end up losing him. And who knows? Something might happen even now, but I'm taking the leap and using this time to be as happy as ever."

Danielle swallowed, trying to dislodge the sudden lump that formed. "I'm so happy for you, Becca. Really. I know how hard it was for you after the accident."

Becca reached her hands forward, taking Danielle's hands in hers. "Thank you. But I'm here if you need to talk about anything or anyone."

"Well, I got fired." That was a surefire way to derail the conversation. The moment the words were out, she regretted the decision. She'd been hoping to wait until after the honeymoon. "Just, don't tell anyone, okay? I don't want my mom to know yet. Or the rest of the town for that matter."

"What? Why?" Becca's mouth dropped open.

Laughing a bit, Danielle said, "I attended a protest because the city council had authorized dumping at one of the lakes near Anaheim. I'm usually careful to stay on the inside so I don't get photographed, but things shifted quickly when a fight broke out, and there was a big picture of me on the front page of the LA Daily the next morning. I can't be the face of neutrality if I'm seen taking sides." The words weren't her own, the slight Southern accent of her former boss shining through.

"Oh, Dani. I'm so sorry. What are you going to do now?"

Danielle stretched her arms in the air, giving her some time to formulate a response. She thought about telling Becca about her alter ego and the books circulating around Sage Creek, but her wedding was coming up in four days, and she could already see the worry in Becca's face. She didn't need to rock the boat just yet.

"I'll figure something out. For now, I'll help out my mom around the house."

"I know that's not your ultimate dream, but I'm sure your mother will be grateful to have you around for longer than a few hours." Becca stuffed the binder into her bag and then said, "Are you ready? We need to head over to Bridal Bliss. Susie said she'd stay a bit later to get your dress fitted."

Danielle stopped mid-bite, the ice cream dripping down the side of her mouth. Wiping it off with a napkin, she glared at Becca. "You didn't tell me that was the reason I needed to meet you today."

"You didn't want to see your best friend after all the time you've been away?" Becca's voice sounded innocent, but her friend knew her too well. "I knew you wouldn't come if I told you outright. Let's go. Susie's been waiting for fifteen minutes already."

Groaning, Danielle left some cash on the table and slid out of the booth. Of all the things she'd sacrificed to be at this wedding, this was not something she wanted to do. She was so used to the power suits for her job, and she'd always been somewhat of a tomboy, preferring t-shirts and jeans to the more girly things Becca preferred. And most of the dresses were made out of tulle or other itchy fabrics she couldn't name. But it was finally time for Becca's happily ever after, and Danielle could sacrifice comfort for at least twelve hours.

CHAPTER 5

*L*iam left a sign on the bookstore door Tuesday afternoon, the same one he used every day he had to pick up Cari from school. The wind blew down from the pond, and he made a mental note to start wearing a jacket now that the weather was turning.

He'd received a call from the hospital that Kara had woken up but that they were still waiting a few days to see if the radiation had helped with any leftover cells. He'd wanted to call her right after, but he pictured his niece's face puckering, saying something about not waiting for her. With all the things she'd been protected from after losing her father when she was very young, it was near impossible to shield her from this disease. Especially if things didn't work out and Kara started to decline.

But he couldn't think about that right now. He had to be positive, or Cari would work out that something was wrong, even though right now things were good.

He stood in his usual spot outside the chain-link fence surrounding the school, enjoying the view of the mountains in the background.

"How's it going today?" a familiar deep voice asked.

Liam turned to see Tanner and Colton walking up behind him. He smiled at the two of them, grateful for their friendship since he'd come to town. Tanner had invited him along to a few things, making the transition easier than Liam expected when he'd first arrived.

"Oh, you know. Just waiting for Cari. She's always the last kid out of the building."

The doors opened, and several of the kids came running out, backpacks and papers in hand as they made their way to the various exits on the property. Of course, Cari was still nowhere among them.

"What are you two up to?" Liam asked.

Colton stuffed his hands into his pants pocket and shifted his weight to one foot. "We've got to put together a few things for the ceremony this weekend."

"Danielle called and said the ceremony is going to be up by the pond instead of in the rec center." Tanner said the words like it was a done deal. "It's going to take whatever spare time we have to get it done."

"What about the bachelor party?" Liam asked, grinning at Colton.

Colton shook his head. "No need for that. My idea of a bachelor party would be the three of us watching a football game. But we can turn one on while we work on this so Danielle doesn't come after us."

Danielle, Mrs. Holloway's daughter. Liam's mind turned, wondering how a woman who'd just barely come to town could have so much sway with these two. Then again, he remembered the feisty nature he'd seen when she retorted against the Crestview woman.

Liam stepped away from the fence, folding his arms over his chest. "We're doing this because Danielle asked?"

Tanner and Colton turned to each other and laughed louder than Liam had heard in a while.

"Danielle is Becca's best friend and maid of honor. Becca told her she really wants the ceremony up by the pond, that the wedding planner is the one who kept pushing for the rec center," Tanner said. "She just uses a little more force when requesting things."

"The pond is important to Becca, and if that's where she wants to get married, we'll make it happen. I've been hoping she'd say something. That wedding planner we hired has been a nightmare to work with." Colton's eyes glazed over as he stared over Liam's shoulder.

Liam nodded, still not getting a real answer to his question. "What does Danielle do? Someone said something about her traveling the world."

"She's a media correspondent in LA," Tanner said. "They send her all over to cover things for the station. I think the last place she reported from was the hurricane in Florida. At least, that's what her mom told me."

"Sounds adventurous." Liam couldn't think of anything else to say, but the fact that she was a public figure, even if only for Los Angeles, was a good enough reason for him to stay away. He'd had enough drama after dealing with his ex-girlfriend, the lover of all things fame. After what she'd done to try and gain more fame, he was better off being the bachelor bookstore owner in this small town.

Cari finally emerged, chatting with her teacher. That was Cari, the girl with all the questions. He smiled as the teacher ushered her outside and waved goodbye.

"Good luck building whatever it is you're building," Liam said, waving to Cari as she crossed the schoolyard. "I'll come help when the store is closed."

Tanner and Colton nodded, walking up Main Street in the direction of the pond.

When Cari reached him, Liam swooped her up into a hug and turned, carrying her down the road a bit. "How was school today?"

"It was a rough day for our class. That's what our teacher said. We all had to clip down on our behavior chart a few times for not listening, but then I helped the teacher and she let me clip back up. I got a prize because of it." The words tumbled out of her like she'd been waiting all day to tell him. "How's the bookstore? Did you sell a lot of books today?"

Liam nodded. "A good amount. We had one of the book clubs in, and they bought a bunch of stuff."

"We're going to the park, right?" Cari asked, walking beside him now, her hand in his. They turned right onto Fourth Street in the direction of the bigger park on that side of town. She tugged on his arm and gave him her best begging face, her lip jutted out and puppy-dog eyes in full effect.

"We can head there for a bit. The hospital said your mom woke up, so we can call her in a little bit. Then I've got to get back to the store, and you need to get your homework done."

Cari groaned next to him. He usually scolded her for it, but his eyes caught on the girl from the bookstore walking with Becca, both coming in their direction.

"Hey, Liam," Becca called, waving.

"How are you today, Becca?" Liam asked, stopping a few feet short of the two women.

Becca grinned. "Doing well. Just taking Danielle here to get fitted for her maid of honor dress."

Danielle was standing a few inches behind her, and she grimaced, looking as if that was the last thing she wanted to do.

Liam couldn't keep a smile from his lips, almost taunting her. "Maid of honor, huh? I guess we'll be seeing each other at the wedding, then."

The woman's eyebrows cinched together, and he could see the curiosity brimming in her eyes. "You've been invited?"

Becca's laugh broke their gaze. "He's one of the groomsmen." She pointed to Liam like that was a perfectly logical explanation when it was kind of surprising to himself. It wasn't like he'd grown up with Colton or had worked with him at one point. But living in Sage Creek had its peculiarities, and becoming good friends with a guy in only six months didn't seem like such a stretch anymore.

"Oh," Danielle said, her mouth forming the letter. She glanced to his side and bent a little bit, saying, "And who is this?"

"I'm Cari." Cari pointed to herself proudly, causing the three adults to chuckle.

"She's my niece. I promised her she could play at the park after school for a bit, so we're heading over to that one." He pointed just past the diner.

Becca grabbed Danielle's arm. "Well, we'll let you two get to the swings, then. Those were always my favorite." She said the last words to Cari.

The little girl bounced on her toes excitedly. "Me too. I love going high."

"The swings are the best. Building a sandcastle is pretty great too," Danielle said, her smile lighting up her face as she spoke to Cari.

His niece tugged on his arm. "Can we make a castle? Can we?" she begged.

"I'll see what I can do," he said, his eyes locked on Danielle's. There was something there that intrigued him, like she was a mystery he had to solve.

Their gaze broke when Becca pulled Danielle in the direction of Bridal Bliss and a thread of disappointment flowed through Liam.

"Good luck with the fitting. We'll see you around." He didn't glance back as they walked away, reminding himself that Danielle Holloway was in the public eye and there was no way she would be staying in this sleepy town longer than she had to.

CHAPTER 6

Danielle wiggled into the dress Becca had picked out for her, wishing she could be at the park with Cari instead. She'd always loved kids, and there were many times when she didn't feel like she'd grown up at all. Plus, there was something about Uncle Liam that made her want to ask him all the questions and figure out who he truly was. His baby-blue eyes pulled her in, and she was starting to feel flutters in her stomach. That hadn't happened since high school and she needed her body to cooperate, to not start feeling things for a guy she barely knew.

Pushing him out of her mind, she focused on the dress. The amount of tulle and beads on the bodice sent off warning signals in her brain, telling her she was going to be uncomfortable for as long as she had to wear it.

It had to be tulle.

Once the dress was on and zipped up, she looked at herself in the mirror. "I look like a purple cupcake," she muttered.

"I heard that!" Becca's voice came from beyond the curtain. "Come out and let me see it."

Danielle kept her arms raised, hoping to avoid the scratchy tulle. She opened the curtain and spun, knowing Becca would make her do it anyway.

"You look beautiful. Why do you look like you want to shoot me?"

Trying to decide if she should just be agreeable, Danielle finally said, "Is there a dress that would work with less of the stuff bound to give me hives?"

As if just realizing it, Becca's eyes flew wide. "Oh, Danielle. I forgot about the fabric. The rest of the bridesmaids are wearing a more simple dress. We could do something else to make you stand out a bit more as the maid of honor."

Danielle nodded. "As long as I won't want to scratch my eyes out the entire time wearing it, I'll do it. Just save me from the tulle." She smiled, hoping Becca would see she was teasing a bit. If there were no other options, she'd just grin and bear it.

"Let me go get Lucy. Susie said she would know where everything is while she's gone."

Turning back to the dressing room, Danielle removed the purple fluff as quickly as possible, grateful for the relief. She'd always had sensitive skin, but with lotion and the right clothes, she'd been able to keep things from flaring up on a regular basis. She just wished she'd brought some cream in her purse to quell the itch beginning in her forearms.

Becca peeked in, stretching out a deep purple satin dress. "See how this one fits."

Danielle looked at the dress. Satin was better, but it would've been nice to have a knit dress for the occasion. Also not appropriate for a wedding. She unzipped the back and stepped one foot into the cool fabric. Better already.

"So, what do you think of Liam?" Becca asked through the curtain.

Danielle's foot caught as she placed the other foot into the dress, and she had to catch herself on the wall so she didn't face-plant in the ground.

"What do you mean? I've met the guy for a total of two minutes." Not entirely true. Maybe ten. Trying to steer the conversation in a different direction, Danielle asked, "He's a groomsman, though, huh?"

"Yeah, Colton doesn't have too many people from his past to invite, and he, Tanner, and Liam have gotten pretty close since they moved to Sage Creek. He's a good guy."

Zipping up the back of the dress as high as she could, she stepped out, giving another twirl.

Becca clapped her hands together. "Oh, that looks perfect on you. We can get them to add a few embellishments, and you'll look amazing. Maybe you'll catch someone's eye." She winked.

Danielle groaned. "I'm currently off the market."

"Oh really? Who's the guy?" Becca asked, not looking convinced.

"Myself. I'm taking time to reflect on my life at the moment." She paused, Liam's light hair and strong jaw making an appearance in her mind. "Can I get out of this thing?" she asked, moving her fingers up and down in front of the dress. Anything to get herself to stop thinking of the attractive bookstore owner.

Becca nodded, but she wasn't giving up on the conversation. "You should get to know Liam. I feel like you two would have a lot in common." Becca's voice came out more of a sing-song.

Danielle knew that tactic all too well. She pulled on her shirt and jeans before walking out with the dress draped over one arm. "I know I don't have a job at the moment, but I doubt I'll be sticking around here long enough to make it worth it."

She could date him, but then she'd be left with that same old guilt once she had to pack up and leave for another assignment. There had always been plenty of that as her mother tried to smile whenever Danielle had to jet off to some new country. But would she be able to handle it from someone not directly related to her?

She handed the dress to the young assistant of the dress shop, grateful that the dress fit well enough to avoid the pins and needles part.

"Sage Creek isn't the worst place to be, Dani. You might find yourself surprised by how life can be here." Becca must have seen Danielle's eye roll because she waved her hands in front of her. "I know there's a lot that goes into you being you, but maybe give it a chance for a couple of weeks. Take a break. Work on something you've wanted to do or finish for a while but haven't had time for because you've been so busy. It might be the real passion you've been looking for."

Danielle stared at her friend, the words tumbling around in her brain. "Says the girl who's got her entire year planned out."

Becca tipped her head back and laughed. "Yes, but I'm not you. Maybe something different will be good for you. And anyway, Colton has been getting me to be more spontaneous. I even let you cross things off my pre-wedding-activities list. Do you have any idea how hard that was for me?"

The two of them laughed as they walked out the door. The sky was dim, filled with gray clouds and the threat of rain.

"I sure hope this storm leaves before Saturday," Danielle said as they walked toward Main Street.

Throwing her hands up, Becca said, "Well, at least we've still got the rec center reserved. It would just mean so much more if we could say our vows by the pond."

Danielle rolled her lips in, not knowing whether to laugh

or cry. Love had never been big for Danielle since everyone she'd known, aside from her mother, had left her at some point. She'd get through this wedding and hope that by some miracle she'd get hired on again, even if it was somewhere she had to work her way up again. Distance from the deeper feelings kept her safe, balanced even.

After saying goodbye to Becca, she walked slowly up Main Street, thinking about her best friend's advice. It had been at least two years since she'd released the last of her cozy mysteries. Maybe it was time to continue the series.

CHAPTER 7

Wednesday rolled around, and Liam had already dropped Cari off at school. Since business tended to be slower on Wednesdays, he usually opened the store later, getting most of his errands run.

They'd been able to video chat with Kara the night before, and although she appeared weak and tired, Cari had talked of nothing else since. Liam just hoped all the surgeries and procedures would be worth it, that Kara would be able to come home and recover. She'd been there through so many of his harder moments, and the thought of losing her wasn't something he wanted to dwell on, for himself or for Cari.

After grocery shopping and taking the mail to the post office, Liam walked over to the newspaper. He'd seen in the last issue that they were looking for a copy editor and was interested in the position. It had been a while since he'd done anything like it, but with a minor in English and having worked on his college newspaper all four years, he hoped it was like riding a bike, maybe with a few courses to brush up.

"Hey, Clyde. How are things today?" he asked the chief editor sitting at the front desk.

"Another day at the office. Lucy had an appointment this morning, so I'm trying to cover the phones while she's gone. I have to say, she does a better job than I do. How that gal manages to work here and at the bridal shop and still keep everything together is beyond me." He leaned forward, rubbing his thumb and pointer finger over his forehead. "I haven't been able to get any work done with all of the calls coming in. Most of them are for a cat that was stuck in the tree for an hour. Three people have called to ask if we'd send a photographer over to take pictures while the fire volunteers rescued it."

Liam laughed and nodded. "I guess it's good that nothing too crazy happens in this town, right?"

Clyde shook his head. "Something a little more exciting than a stranded cat would definitely make my job a little more enjoyable. What can I help you with?"

"I saw the ad that said you were looking for a copy editor. I thought I'd apply." Liam stuck one hand in his pant pocket, keeping eye contact with the man in front of him.

Clyde's eyes squinted a bit, his pointer finger tapping along his lips. An awkward pause settled between them, and Liam glanced around, wondering if he'd missed something.

"Sorry, just got lost in thought. I have an application you can fill out, and we'll see if you're qualified."

Raising his eyebrow, Liam asked, "You have that many people wanting the job, huh?"

The larger man had stood and turned toward another office, but he stopped and faced Liam. With a wide smile, he said, "What qualifications do you have, then, son?"

Liam listed off his time as the business manager and copy editor for his high school paper, then as the chief editor for his college paper. The minor in English he threw in as a bonus, and the man's eyes grew wider with each announcement. As an investment banker, he hadn't used those skills as much, which meant he would need to find an online class or two to enroll in.

"Well, Liam, you're hired. The gal we had before is out on maternity leave, and she said she probably won't be coming back if we can find someone to take over. You can get started today. Let me run and get the job description packet for you from my office. Will you watch the phones for a minute?" The man turned before Liam had time to give him an answer.

Taking a seat, Liam interlaced his fingers and rested them on the back of his head. The thrill of something else to keep him occupied during the slow times at the bookstore made it all the sweeter.

The door opened, and as Danielle walked in, he dropped his arms, slamming his funny bone on the desk. He grimaced, the odd sensation flowing through his arm to his fingertips.

"Are you all right?" Danielle walked up to him, resting her purse on the top of the raised desk.

"Yep," he said through clenched teeth. The pain was easing up, and he tried to smile.

She flashed him a half-smile. "You work at the paper too?"

Liam laughed and grinned. "I was hired on about fifteen seconds ago. I'm just supposed to cover the phone while Clyde is in back looking for something. What are you here for?" He turned his head to give her a look out of the corner of his eye.

She lifted her head, scanning the office windows behind Liam. "I just had something to ask Clyde. He's here, right?"

He could hear her foot tapping and wasn't sure what to say, when Clyde came out front, a stack of papers in his hands.

Clyde looked up a moment and smiled when he saw Danielle. "Our own famous reporter, coming back to her old haunt. What can I do for you, Dani?"

Liam noticed how her chin raised and a wide smile crossed her face, lighting up her eyes. She seemed to be pretending Liam wasn't there, and he laughed inwardly. The girl had spunk.

"I'll be in town for several weeks, maybe longer, and I was wondering if I can help out in any way. Write an editorial here and there. Maybe cover some of the events. I'll go crazy just hanging out at my mother's house."

Turning to look at Clyde's face, Liam knew the answer, and he wished he'd brought popcorn because sparks were going to fly.

"Sam took over the headlines when you left. I'm sorry, Dani." He looked down at the papers in his hand and then up at her again. He moved his gaze from Liam to Danielle several times. "I've just had a thought about something, though. What would you think about an op-ed piece?"

Danielle and Liam both pointed to themselves and said, "Me?" at the same time. Liam chuckled when he saw daggers flying in his direction from Danielle.

"You own a bookstore, and suddenly you're a writer?" Her voice was clipped, and her cheeks turned a deep shade of red. She must not be used to sharing a story.

Liam thought of the difference of the Danielle he'd bumped into on the street when taking Cari to the park. Was this version of her threatened by him?

Standing, Liam towered over her even from behind the desk. "I happen to be a good writer. I was on the newspaper in college and have written a few articles for other publications since."

Danielle scoffed. "Just because you survived a college paper doesn't mean you're up for journalism."

He couldn't help chuckling at her irritation. "It's a small town. As long as it makes Velda happy, I think I'll be okay. I don't think I'll survive long if she withholds her Oreo shakes from me."

Danielle's shoulders relaxed, and a small smile formed. "You're right about that. Keep Velda happy, and life can be a lot easier around here." Her tone signaled there was at least one story that fit into that category for her.

Clyde raised his hands in between the two of them. "Okay, children. Do I need to send you to time out?" The half-smile he gave them and the look of disdain from Danielle was enough for one night. Liam needed to keep his mouth shut or he really was going to be on her don't-speak-to list.

"What I'm proposing will be interesting, seeing the sparks fly between you two. But I think the town would love something witty and raw, which is where you come in. I'm thinking a 'His & Hers' column."

Liam wrinkled his nose. "A what?"

Danielle only shook her head, not acknowledging Liam's question. "No, let me do it. I've got plenty of ideas for editorials. Subscriptions will go through the roof."

Liam noticed the negotiating tone to her voice and laughed, drawing her ire.

Clyde shook his head. "No. I want it to be both of you. You'll get together and come up with a topic, writing the guy's and girl's point of view on it. We'll need to make sure it's nothing too crazy. We are a family-friendly newspaper, you know."

Sticking his hand out to Clyde, Liam said, "I'm in. Sounds like a great challenge."

They shook hands, and Liam turned to Danielle. "Who knows? Maybe I'll learn a thing or two from our resident expert."

Danielle closed her eyes and took in a deep breath. When

she opened them, he noticed they seemed almost teal, and it caused him to look closer.

"Fine. I'll do it. When do you want it?"

"I'll give you a week on this first one. Send me your finalized pieces by next Thursday, and I'll run them in the weekend edition."

Danielle nodded and turned on her heel, walking out the door.

Liam thanked Clyde and then jogged a bit to catch up with her. "I hope I didn't steal your thunder in there." Although, he'd liked the pointed jabs she'd thrown at him.

She turned and glared at him. "Really? Because it looked like you were enjoying every minute."

"I look forward to our article. Do you have a topic in mind?"

For once, her face softened, and he was surprised at how soft her skin looked. Shaking her head, she said, "Let me think about it. We can discuss it at the wedding."

"You want to discuss writing an article at your best friend's wedding?" Liam had thought she was a bit intense, but he hadn't realized she was that devoted to her work.

Frowning, she shrugged. "You're right. I'll probably be running errands all day for Becca. We can meet at the diner on Sunday."

He tried to hold in a chuckle, but her ears perked up, and she turned to look at him. "What's so funny?"

"The diner is closed on Sundays." He wondered how long it had been since she'd actually been home. But it seemed like the diner had always had the same hours of operation. Maybe she just wasn't thinking clearly.

She opened her mouth to say something and then closed it with a humbled expression. "Okay, the park, then. Bring your own lunch."

"Sounds good. See you then."

For some reason, Liam couldn't wait. This was going to be more fun than he'd thought when he walked into the newspaper office that morning. With Cari around, he wasn't bored often, but a little teasing of the town reporter could make things even more interesting.

The next evening, Danielle was more than ready for this bridal shower to be over. At the suggestion of her mother, she'd spent most of the night before coming up with games to entertain the guests. Thank goodness for Clip Board so she could keep a bunch of her ideas online and go through them after. She'd settled all the food with Velda after leaving the newspaper office.

The newspaper. She replayed the interaction she'd had with Liam and the giddy look he gave her when they'd agreed to have lunch. For some reason, his flashy smile and perfect teeth pushed several of her buttons.

She needed to forget about him, needed to focus on the task at hand, which was pulling off a shower for her best friend.

She'd spent the morning with her mother and Dottie Watkins, decorating the gazebo in the park. They'd ordered several dozen flowers from Becca under the guise that it would be used for an event at the city offices. The three of them had worked the flowers into the table decorations and around the poles of the gazebo.

"How can I help?" a deep voice asked from behind her.

Danielle turned, still holding the napkins she'd been arranging on the table, to find the guy she'd been trying to forget.

"Umm," she tried to stall, glancing around the park to see what still needed to be done. "You could get out the Jenga game if you want. Just set it on the table right over there." She pointed to a small rectangular table to her left.

Liam stepped over to the table, picking up the box. "Jenga, huh? I haven't played this game in a while. What are you using it for tonight?"

Danielle finished with the napkins and grabbed a handful of forks from the box, placing them in the wire holder she'd borrowed from her mom. With the white table-cloths and the bits of purple, the park didn't look half bad considering she'd begun most of it twenty-four hours before.

She pointed to the game Liam had unboxed and was steadily trying to keep in a single tower. "That is for Doubles Jenga."

He laughed, knocking over a few of the pieces as he tried to add more. "What other games did you have in mind?"

Danielle sank into a folding chair next to one of the tables. It had been a long day, and she needed a rest.

"Bingo based on what gifts you think will be given, bride and groom trivia," she said, pulling out a piece of paper from her back pocket. She scanned her writing, trying to remember the last of it. "There is also a 'guess how much candy is in the jar' and sharing favorite date ideas for the couple."

With one eyebrow raised, Liam smirked. "Is this what most bridal showers are like?"

"It's been a while since I've been to any, let alone one where the guys are invited. I just went with some ideas I found online." She folded her paper back up and pulled out her phone. Fifteen minutes. "Where is Cari?"

"Playing at the neighbor's. She asked about you earlier, wondering if you could come help build a sandcastle."

"What did you say?" Danielle tilted her head to one side, curious to hear his answer.

Liam's bright teeth shined through his smile. "I just said we'd have to ask you the next time we saw you."

Talking floated to her ears, and she turned, seeing several of the ladies of Sage Creek walking in their direction. The sooner everyone showed up, the faster this thing would be done.

"Was this a surprise for the happy couple?" Liam asked, reminding her that he was behind her.

"Mayor Watkins is going to lure them over with some story about needing repairs to the gazebo and ideas on what flowers to grow in the park gardens." Danielle stood, smoothing out her shirt. She walked over to the long table, moving one of the large vases of flowers for the food that would be coming.

Liam nodded, the corner of his mouth turning up a fraction. "Sounds like the mayor."

Danielle found herself staring at him for longer than was acceptable, and when he caught her, she looked away, pretending to fix the tablecloth on the large table. What was her deal? Just because he was attractive didn't mean she needed to feed those feelings anymore. She'd be the one left hurting in the end.

Becca and Colton came with the mayor as expected, their excitement and surprise something Danielle was happy about. It was hard to spring anything on her best friend, but at least she was giddy about the event.

After they'd eaten the sandwiches, salads, and desserts Velda had sent with some of her staff, Danielle stood, ready to play the games. It was strange addressing more than just the cameraman, and with the number of people there, she had to take a breath before saying anything.

"We're excited to have you all here to celebrate Becca and Colton. We've got a few games to play before we have them open gifts." She pointed to the table heaped with wrapped boxes and gift bags. She went over the games at different stations, her nerves feeling raw as she hoped the guests would enjoy them. Once she finished, she said, "Pair up with someone, and we'll get started."

People began milling about, and from a quick look, all the guys had been paired up, leaving a group of the older women sitting around one of the tables chatting. Danielle strolled over to them, loving the happiness on her mother's face as she laughed at something one of the ladies had said.

"Aren't you ladies going to join the games?"

Velda waved her hand. "Honey, we've played enough games in our lifetime. We'll leave it to you young people. From the looks of things over there, it seems you're on the road to being a matchmaker, Danielle." She pointed in the direction of the six couples milling about the tables. Several looked like they were enjoying each other's company.

Danielle laughed, walking back over to the table of food. She could use another chicken salad sandwich.

"Party planner isn't going to participate in the festivities?" Liam asked, stepping up to the table across from her.

"I had hoped that planning this was like a get-out-of-activity-free card." She took a bite of the sandwich without moving her gaze from his face.

Liam lifted his hand and waved his fingers, beckoning her. "Let's go. Who knows? We might have fun."

Danielle glanced at the Jenga game where the couple at the table giggled as they tried to remove a block from the tower. The idea was to tie their hands together, making them have to talk to get the block out successfully.

She shook her head. "I'm good. I—"

"Oh, come on, Dani. It will be fun." Becca bumped into Danielle with her hip, sending her off-balance.

Danielle caught herself on the table before she fell and sent a glare in Becca's direction once she'd recovered.

She and Liam started with the candy-jar guessing and then filled out their gift bingo cards, not saying much during that time. Danielle wasn't sure whether to be annoyed or happy that he'd asked to be her partner.

Doubles Jenga was next, and they were challenging Becca and Colton, who seemed to be on a winning streak.

Liam picked up the handkerchief Danielle had brought for tying their hands together. "Right hand or left?"

"I can do either. Which do you prefer?"

"I'll take the left." He lifted his hand next to Danielle's right, causing the hairs around her wrist to stand on end. When his skin touched hers, she jumped when she felt the shock of it.

"Sorry," she said. Liam had been tying the handkerchief, but she'd pulled it loose.

Liam looked up, his hooded eyes causing a deeper attraction to rise in her. She had to turn her gaze away, looking in the direction of the older ladies. When she realized they were all watching her, she closed her eyes, feeling embarrassment heat to the tips of her ears.

"Ready?" Liam's voice caused her eyes to snap open, and she nodded. She could handle a few minutes attached to this guy. It wasn't like it would be forever.

Danielle nodded, shifting closer to the table with Liam.

"Another pair of competitors. We've got them, right, dear?" Colton said, kissing Becca's temple.

"Definitely." Becca's confident smile only enhanced Danielle's competitiveness.

"We'll see about that," Danielle said, looking to Liam for his answer. His laid-back expression wasn't helping her emotions stay under control, and her heartbeat sped up.

Becca and Colton went first, successfully placing their piece on the top of the tower.

"Use your finger to push one of the middle pieces," Danielle said, whispering to Liam. They were so close to each other, her lips only inches from his.

Liam moved their hands closer to the tower, sticking out his pointer finger to test a few of the pieces. "I'll push, and you pull it out," he said, focusing on the block.

Danielle waited until he was done and guided their hands over the tower. It took a few moments to figure out how to grab the block with their hands tied together, but she was able to get it without pulling down any extra pieces. She went to place it on top, when Liam's phone rang. He shifted to grab it, pulling their connected hands over the top of the tower and toppling the blocks to the table.

Liam's expression flickered a wave of emotions, and he said, "I'm so sorry. I just need to get this." He moved his left hand again, pulling Danielle with him.

"Let me help you with that." Danielle worked her finger and thumb into the knot around their wrists, freeing them from the handkerchief.

"Thanks. Just give me a minute, and we'll finish the games." His eyes were more pleading that she was used to, but she brushed it off as he moved away.

"I think the two of you look good together." Becca's voice sounded like she was singing notes for a warm-up concert.

Danielle shook her head, walking back over to her uneaten sandwich. Maybe with time away from Liam, she could get her pulse to return to normal.

CHAPTER 9

*L*iam felt bad about losing the game, especially when he could see how much Danielle wanted to win. Playing the games with her had been fun, and he'd been able to read even more about her. She was highly competitive but had a sort of people-pleaser attitude about her.

He'd set up a certain ringtone for the hospital, and when it had sounded, he'd lost his focus, hoping nothing had gone wrong with his sister.

"Mr. Pearson, this is Dr. Grant over in Grand Junction. The radiation helped get rid of some of the cells, but we found a few more tumors in her leg. It's not safe to do surgery again just yet, but we think it will be best to do another round of radiation to see if we can reduce their size."

"Do it."

"These tumors are usually resistant to this kind of treatment, but we can try—"

"We know. Just do it. My sister wants whatever time she can have with her daughter. If this will help her get better faster than waiting another several weeks or months for the tumors to grow, do it."

Liam ran his hand over his face. He hung up the call, wishing they'd been able to tell him a date they could work toward for Kara's release. Cari was doing okay, but it would be nice to have her mother back.

He looked back at the party where Colton and Becca were opening presents together. A dull ache formed in his chest, the feeling that had come more and more often over the past several weeks. The engaged couple had a bright future ahead of them. All Liam had wanted was to have someone at his side, but the chances of losing her were higher than he was comfortable with. After losing his parents, his brother-in-law, and possibly his sister, he wasn't sure he could take any more heartbreak.

On that thought, his eyes turned to rest on Danielle, his curiosity triggering several alarm warnings in his mind. Was she worth the risk? His brain kept telling him he didn't want to find out.

CHAPTER 10

*D*anielle wished she had wings to fly all over town on Friday as she was busy finalizing last-minute details for the wedding. They'd successfully convinced the wedding planner to have the wedding ceremony up near the reservoir above the town hall, and Danielle smiled as she remembered the look of dread on the woman's face. She didn't seem to be one for nature, and anytime they were outdoors, she would look around for birds, afraid they'd poop on her.

The bridal shower had been a huge success, and what Becca didn't already have, there were gifts to cover it. The fact that Liam had left suddenly caused Danielle to wonder what had happened. There was still a lot to learn about him, but hours later, she could still feel the electricity in her hand from when they'd been tied together for the game.

Friday morning had been spent helping Colton and Tanner with the gazebo they'd put together up by the pond. The only large section of flat ground big enough to hold chairs for the guests was to the left and tucked up into the mountain a bit. But as the few decorations were set out and the gazebo decorated, Danielle grew excited for the wedding to take place. She just hoped all went well for Becca this time around.

"Do you think the weather will hold out?" a familiar deep voice asked behind her.

Danielle turned slowly, coming face to face with Liam. "We can only hope. What are you doing up here?" Danielle didn't mean for the remark to sound so harsh, like she was shunning an outsider.

It seemed as though the comment just rolled off the man standing in front of her. "I closed the store a bit early. Thought I'd come up and see if the guys could use any more help." He motioned to the gazebo. "That's impressive. Sometimes I wish I had those kinds of craftsman-like skills."

Danielle studied his face, the strong jaw and piercing blue eyes. A tingle zipped through her chest, and she shook it off, knowing it was best not to start down that road. The guy was handsome but irritating, and if she could just remember that, she'd leave this town in a few weeks without any more trouble than she'd arrived with.

But her curiosity got the better of her, and her journalistic persona emerged. "What brought you to Sage Creek?" She glanced at the long-sleeved fitted tee accentuating a trim figure. Runner, maybe?

Liam shifted his weight to his back foot and looked her in the eyes, those blue irises making it hard to look away. "I lived in New York for a few years and just needed a change of pace. My mother always had this dream to open up a bookstore, so my sister and I decided to do that here, in her memory."

"I'm so sorry. I didn't know." A stab of guilt hit her chest. The loss of a parent had been hard for Danielle, and this piece of information drew her in, making her want to know more.

He shook his head and waved off the comment. "It's been a while. Our parents were older when they got married and had the two of us, so it wasn't completely out of the blue when they passed. My dad would be seventy-seven and my mother seventy-five now."

"That's mind-boggling. My mom had me at twenty, so she's only forty-seven now. Although she sometimes acts like she could be retired." Her mother had done a lot to help support Danielle ever since her father walked out, taking jobs at weird hours in order to put food on the table. It aged her much faster than she should have, but Danielle was grateful for it. She just needed to show that gratitude a bit more.

Colton and Tanner grabbed the last of their tools after setting up some of the signs and lanterns needed for the ceremony. Danielle took a few steps to follow and was surprised when she found Liam walking in sync with her.

"Did your sister live here before you moved here?" She took a glance at his face, again feeling some kind of spark in her chest at his profile. She was beginning to see there were many layers to the man next to her, and that kept her intrigued.

"Yeah, she's been here for about seven years. Kara Plumfield."

Danielle stopped and turned to him. "Wait, Kara is your sister?"

He nodded, and they continued on, with Danielle's thoughts racing faster than they had in days. "How is your sister? I haven't seen her in so long."

Kara had always been so kind to Danielle, especially when they'd worked together on one of the holiday events the small town put on. Danielle had come home for a long break from college and had loved getting to know and work with Kara. She'd been horrible at keeping in touch and hadn't reached out as often when her husband passed away.

The look of sadness that crossed his face for mere seconds made her wonder what had happened. He glanced at Danielle again, his mouth open to say something but hesitated as he kept moving down the trail back to town. "She, uh, well, she's got a form of cancer. She just had the bigger tumors removed a few days ago. I got a call while at the shower yesterday that they've found several other places where the tumors spread, so they're going to try and reduce the size with radiation."

Danielle rested her hand lightly on his forearm, pulling him to a stop. She felt that spark between them increase as she gazed into his eyes. "Again, I'm sorry. It seems I'm the last one to know everything that happens in this town anymore. Is there anything I can do to help?"

The corner of Liam's mouth rose, and he shook his head. "We're just waiting to see what else we can do." He leaned forward a bit, causing a woodsy scent to fill her nose. His voice dropped lower before saying, "And you're not the last one to know. She didn't want the whole town to hear of it."

Danielle took a step back, swallowing hard. She was supposed to be keeping her thoughts to a professional level, knowing she couldn't get attached. She'd never wanted to before, but there was something invisible pulling her toward Liam, and the idea of even giving him an inkling of emotion caused her mind to go haywire.

Once they reached the side of the fountain in front of Town Hall, she said, "It was good to talk to you. I better run and see if Becca needs anything before the big day tomorrow. If you need me to watch Cari at all, please don't hesitate to ask. See you later."

The wide grin and short nod from Liam sent her insides flipping, and she nearly ran to get away from him. Staying neutral was going to be harder than expected.

$\mathcal{D}$anielle headed down the street, catching herself before she face-planted, and Liam had to bite his lip to keep from laughing out loud. He'd seen a pothole in the asphalt earlier and wondered if that's what she'd tripped over.

He strolled down the road, taking in the sights and sounds of the fall weather. It had been interesting to watch as the journalist in Danielle had taken over, interrogating him, and yet, as he'd mentioned several little details, it was as though that façade had cracked, showing the more vulnerable side of her. As much as he would've liked to say he felt nothing when she touched his arm, it wasn't that easy. He still felt a warmth where her palm had been, even through the soft cotton of his t-shirt.

And the fact that she'd volunteered to watch Cari for him spoke volumes. His ex-girlfriend, Tawnee, had basically been afraid of any and all children. Looking back now, it was amazing Liam had dated her for as long as he did. But he wanted children, and he just had to find someone who wanted the same thing. Would Danielle be that person?

He walked down the first street on the left and continued a few houses down, where he knocked on the McCready home.

Mrs. McCready's smile dropped as she answered the door. "Oh, Liam. That was short. Cari and I just set up Battleship to play. Are you sure you don't need to do anything else this evening? We can watch her for a few more hours if you need a break."

Liam smiled. "I appreciate that, Mrs. McCready, but we've got a long day of wedding activities tomorrow, and I don't want Cari to be grumpy."

Cari came to the door, her hands clasped together and her begging face on again. "Please, Uncle Liam. Can't we just play this one game?"

Glancing at his phone, Liam frowned. "I would love to stay, but it's already late. We've got to get you in the tub and in bed. But maybe we can call and see how your mom is doing. Does that sound good?"

Nodding, Cari hopped up and down. "When can we go see her again? It's been forever."

"Soon. Help Mrs. McCready pick up the game, and we'll head home." He gave Cari a gentle push toward the living room.

"It's fine. I can put it away. You two head on home, and we'll see you at the wedding tomorrow." Mrs. McCready grinned, pulling Cari in for a hug. "You'll have to come sit with us while Liam gets ready for the wedding." She looked up at Liam. "Send her over if you need to help with anything tomorrow. Cari's no trouble with us."

Emotion clogged his throat, and he could only nod as he stepped back onto the front porch. The people of this town never ceased to amaze him with their kindness. He just hoped he could be like that for someone someday.

"What's wrong?" Cari asked, slipping her hand into his as

they strolled back down the road. She scrunched up her nose, pushing her glasses back up a bit.

Squeezing her hand, Liam grinned at her. "Nothing. I just like this town."

"You don't have to cry about it," she said, now using her pointer finger to slide the glasses onto the bridge of her nose. "But Mom will like hearing that you like living here. She's been worried you'll be bored and want to move back to the city."

"She said that?"

When Cari nodded, he asked, "When?"

"A couple of weeks ago. I just heard her say she hoped you liked it here and didn't regret coming here for us." The way Cari said it, Liam wasn't sure she completely understood the meaning behind it.

He pulled her to a stop and bent down so he was at eye level with his niece. "Just know, I'm not going anywhere, okay? No matter what happens, I'm going to stick around here and bug you all day." He grinned at her as she giggled.

"I'm okay with that. As long as you keep making me pancakes." She gave him a sly side-smile and pulled him up so they could continue walking.

"Deal. Now, let's go see how your mom is doing, shall we?"

* * *

"Hey, sis. How are you?" Liam stared at the pale form on the screen of his phone. Cari had finished talking to her and had headed upstairs to get ready for bed, leaving Liam the ability to speak more freely than if she were still in the room.

It was hard seeing Kara like this, and he wished there was something more proactive he could do. Taking care of Cari helped Kara feel more comfortable, but if only some procedure could speed up the whole process, he would find a way to afford it.

Kara's weak smile looked as though it took all the energy out of her as she dropped it moments later. "I've been better. But they'll start a round of radiation on Monday. Let's just pray my body decides to cooperate." Her chest heaved like she'd spoken too much.

"You'll do great. I'll come to the hospital and be with you through it." He'd just leave the shop closed for the day.

"No." The word was short but said with force. Determination spread over Kara's face.

"It's not a big deal. I can ask someone to watch Cari after school—"

"No." Kara took another big breath before she could speak more. "Stay with Cari. If something happens—"

"We're not going there, Kara." Liam swallowed, trying to block out the emotion that was surfacing. "We're taking this one day at a time. Don't even talk about leaving us."

The room was silent for several moments as tears streaked down both their faces.

"Whatever happens, it will be for the best." Kara's voice was just a whisper.

Liam heard Cari's voice from the stairs asking where the toothpaste had gone. Wiping at the tears, he turned back to the screen. "I've got to help Cari. Don't give up, Kara. Just don't give up. We'll find a way to get you home."

Once he hung up, he sat for an extra few seconds, controlling his emotions. She had to live. He stood, sending up a prayer that they'd find a way to beat the cancer.

CHAPTER 12

Saturday morning felt like a whirlwind. Danielle had come down with a migraine the night before and had gone home before karaoke night, and even though she was in pain, she'd never been more grateful to miss something in her life. Most of the activities Becca had on her list hadn't taken place because of the surprise shower, but karaoke had been a must.

Tara Jones and Carissa Ashby were the two bridesmaids, and they'd all gotten manicures and pedicures at seven Saturday morning, followed by an elaborate hairstyle that made Danielle do a double-take when she looked in the mirror. She'd fallen asleep a few times while Brielle, one of the hairdressers, did her hair. How she'd be able to make it through the ceremony and reception that afternoon and evening without a nap was going to be interesting.

After placing the veil in Becca's half updo, Danielle smoothed it out and then spread the back of the dress out, inspecting every part of it to make sure nothing was amiss. They'd set up a makeshift dressing room in the courtroom at Town Hall, and Danielle stepped back, admiring her friend in her princess-style ball gown. She saw Becca's tears forming and stepped forward again, wrapping her arms around her.

"Shhh. It's all right. Your family is here with you, looking down on this amazing day. And this town is basically kin anyway, so we're all excited to share this with you. Got it?" Danielle pulled back and looked into Becca's eyes.

Becca sniffed, wiping at the corner of her eyes delicately. "Thanks, Dani. I'm glad you came. I don't know what I would have done without you these past few days."

Danielle grabbed a tissue from a box on one of the desks and handed it to her friend. Then she grabbed a few more and stuffed them under her bra strap, hidden in the sleeve of the dress she was wearing. If Becca was already crying, there would definitely be some tears later.

Grinning, Danielle said, "Don't thank me yet. We've still got to get you up the hill with all this fabric." She waved at the length of the dress, and the two of them laughed.

They made their way out the door and started up the trail. Susie had been on her way up to the wedding and volunteered to help hold up the dress, avoiding any mud and dirt.

"How was the out-of-town wedding?" Danielle asked her as they struggled up the hill. While she was grateful Becca had gone for gold flats instead of heels, it was still difficult to find a grip on the trail.

"I survived it. The mother of the bride went a little crazy at the reception last night, but the rest of it went off without a hitch." Susie laughed a bit, and Danielle joined in, wondering what other odd situations the girl had been through as a wedding planner. That could be something interesting for the town newspaper. But that wouldn't work as a two-part article. She'd have to come up with something else she and Liam could write about. She'd almost forgotten about the article after all that had transpired over the past three days.

As they inched their way up, Danielle wished she'd thought to add some stepping stones or something to the trail yesterday when they'd brought the gazebo up to the pond. At one point near the top, Becca slipped but recovered before falling down.

Joking, Danielle said, "Why did you want to get married up here again?"

"Because of that." Becca's arm moved over the scenery as they made it to the crest of the hill. Danielle hadn't taken the time to get a good look at the landscape the day before, as she'd been focused on getting everything ready. But as she looked up at the reds, oranges, and yellows, she couldn't help but feel a measure of peace.

It was idyllic for a wedding, even if that wedding wasn't Danielle's.

They left the bride at the end of a trail of white petals. Dottie Watkins handed Becca and Danielle bouquets of lilies, and Mayor Watkins extended his arm to the bride. Susie found a seat toward the middle of the rows of chairs, and Danielle stepped down the aisle behind the two bridesmaids, the sound of the portable keyboard someone had brought out to play music helping her rhythm.

Danielle stepped into position in front of the gazebo and décor, looking down to swipe off a few pieces of mud that had caught onto her dress. She held her bouquet and looked out over the crowd, smiling at all the familiar faces and some she didn't recognize.

As Becca walked down the aisle, Danielle turned to see Colton's face, and while he looked like a man in love, her attention caught on the man standing behind him. Liam Pearson. Where was Tanner? Wasn't he the best man?

She studied his face, several similarities sticking out

between him and Kara, and she felt guilty once again. Had he come to Sage Creek from New York because of the diagnosis? It would be hard to keep a secret from the town for that long, and she'd only just had the cancer removed a few days before.

Liam turned to look in Danielle's direction and gave her a lazy smile, and she turned her gaze, not willing to break down all the walls she'd set up for herself.

Becca made it to the front of the aisle and handed Danielle her bouquet before turning toward Colton, pulling Danielle away from investigating and back to the present.

Pastor Thurgood opened a book and started to read in his monotone voice. "Dearly beloved, we are gathered here today in this beautiful location to celebrate the union of Colton Maxfield and Rebecca Taylor."

That was as far as Danielle made it before a fly started buzzing in her ear. She tried to swat at it with force but also so that the world watching the scene to her left wouldn't be distracted by her actions. Time and time again, the fly danced around her face, and she wished she could take off her shoe and swat at it. It finally left her alone, and as she watched her friend pledge her life to love the man in front of her, Danielle suddenly wished for the distraction again.

Being the maid of honor when she was so set on avoiding relationships was a lot harder than she'd imagined.

Taking in slow, deep breaths, Danielle tried to focus on what was going on in the ceremony. "Do you, Colton, take Rebecca to be your lawfully wedded wife, to have and to hold, in sickness and in health…"

"With this ring, I thee wed." Becca's voice was all Danielle could hear, and she was grateful the ceremony was nearing its end. The day was unseasonably warm, and Danielle was ready to move out of the line of the rays of sun.

The pastor said, "You may now kiss the bride."

The two of them bent together, and while Danielle was grateful Becca had found someone to love, she couldn't bear to watch them kiss. She'd never been able to watch kisses on TV, let alone in real life. Sure, she'd been kissed several times, but kissing itself was so intimate that it felt like spying.

She focused on a large rock poking out of the ground to her side until the crowd cheered and clapped, signaling the time to look forward once again.

Danielle handed Becca her bouquet and watched as her best friend and her husband walked down the aisle. Things would never be the same. She wouldn't be able to pop into Sage Creek anymore and have unlimited time with Becca. Her friend would have other responsibilities and obligations now that she was hitched. The feeling left a hollow chasm in Danielle's chest, and she worked to take in a breath.

"I believe it's our turn to follow the bride and groom," Liam's soft voice said, his outstretched arm coming into view.

Danielle looked up at him, doing her best to fight back all the emotions building inside. Reaching her hand up, she wrapped it through his arm and let him lead her down the aisle and into the grove of trees leading back to the town.

"Are you all right?" he asked, his voice soft once again.

Danielle licked her lips, the heat suddenly making her thirsty. "Yes, it's just different when people get married. It's like everything you knew before will never be the same again."

"True. I've known Colton for, like, six months," he said, a bright smile on his face again with the small joke, "and he's a really good guy." He paused again, and she could feel his curiosity as he opened and closed his mouth a few times.

She dropped her hand once they were through the trees and walking down the dirt path. "Out with it," she said when he didn't say anything.

He looked at her with a mixture of surprise and amusement. "I just noticed you didn't stare at the couple while they were kissing. I thought watching mushy love stories and happy endings was something all girls loved to do."

Danielle shook her head and focused on the ground in front of her, hoping she wouldn't trip with him next to her. Being at his side seemed to put her body on edge, and she needed to put on the brakes before things got out of hand.

"I like all that stuff. I did buy four romance novels from you the other day." She laughed at him, wishing the charge of air between them would stop increasing. It was hard to concentrate. "I just—I don't know. It's weird watching other people kiss; don't you think?" She raised an eyebrow and smiled when Liam started laughing. That wasn't the only reason, but she wasn't ready to go too deep into her beliefs about a relationship and marriage.

"I guess I'd never really thought about it, but that could be a good point for our joint article." He flashed her a smile, and Danielle turned her head, not wanting to stare.

After making it to the bottom of the path, she shook her head. "No, just like you said, most women like to watch stuff like that, and I do not. We'll need something better, something that will get the town talking."

"A true journalist. How long do you think you'll be in town?" It might have been some strange wish, but Danielle thought she saw more than curiosity in his face when he asked the question.

Danielle rolled in her bottom lip and nodded. "I'm in the middle of a job change, and I'm pretty sure I'll be starting from scratch, unless by some miracle I can write a book about my life and it makes the bestseller list." She chuckled, the sound coming from deep down. If only it were that easy to sell books. Then again, she was still surprised by the surge of interest in her cozy mysteries.

"Why not? I'm sure you've had plenty of adventures in your life. Why not write a book so people can learn about those places through you?" Liam's hands were stuffed into his suit pants pockets, and he looked serious, causing Danielle to take a step back. Man, he filled out that suit coat well.

No one had ever really understood her writing interests. Her mother had been loyal to the grocery store since they'd moved to Sage Creek when Danielle was three. She vaguely remembered her father, and most of her friends in this small town were practical, knowing that selling a service or holding a position in the town would bring in x amount of money.

To a certain extent, she'd been like that with her job, but it wasn't enough just to find out a little information. She'd always gone overboard. She'd been given crazy looks more often than she cared to admit, which was probably why she didn't want to tell anyone about MK Malone's true identity just yet, if ever.

She caught Liam staring at her and tried to remember what he'd asked. Oh yes, a book about herself. "Maybe when I'm old and gray and I know the outcome of the story. But not yet. There are still too many variables in play to make a concise judgment on my life."

"Hmmm." Liam tapped his finger against his lips, his other arm bent to support the elbow.

"What are you *hmmm*ing about?"

"I just didn't picture you as having that much vision about life. I took you for a live-in-the-moment kind of girl. You know, the ones who just go wherever and whenever they want and don't have any set goals for the future?"

Danielle glared at him, her chest rising and falling rapidly as irritation bubbled in her stomach. "I'll have you know, I have plenty of goals for the future. But of course, you're just like every other person in the world who thinks that the goals everyone has have to be accomplished by a certain age. Well, maybe I'm not ready for what everyone expects just yet. I might never be."

"That's it." Liam snapped his fingers and then raised both arms in the air as though he'd made a field goal.

"What are you talking about? Did you not just hear what I was saying?" The anger in Danielle simmered, threatening to explode.

With both hands on his hips, Liam smiled, looking down at her from his slightly taller form. "That can be the topic of our editorial. We can talk about the things society thinks we should be doing at certain ages and what we really feel about that."

Danielle wanted to say something snarky, but it seemed like every way she looked at the idea, she couldn't find any holes in it. "Okay, I can get behind that one. I'm sure everyone will just *love* what we have to say about it."

Liam's face turned serious, his eyebrows cinching together. "You're not going to use this piece as some platform to promote a man-hating agenda to Sage Creek, right?"

With her jaw dropped open, Danielle hesitated, trying to figure out how to respond to his accusation. "I can't believe you'd say that. What gave you that impression?"

"Just because you are new in town doesn't mean you don't have a reputation. Some of the people in this town have followed every story and every piece you've ever written, and from brushing up on them the past few days, that's the impression I got."

Grinding her molars together, Danielle wished she was at least six inches taller so she didn't have to tip her head back so far to look at him. This was when she'd love to have heels. "You looked me up on the internet?"

He shrugged. "I was curious, especially since we'll be

writing together. And there's no better way to get to know someone than through their passions."

Danielle stood there, unable to speak or even conjure enough words to make a sentence. A guy was curious about her and had taken the time to research her. She wanted to be flattered, but the part about man-hating popped to the front of her thoughts.

"What happened to Tanner?" she asked, taking a step away so the hint of his cologne wouldn't mess with her head.

"He got sick from some food he ate last night. Colton asked me to fill in as the best man."

That meant she would have to spend more one-on-one time with Liam tonight. The thought made the mixture of feelings in her stomach lurch.

"I think I forgot a few things for the reception. I'll, uh, see you there."

"You're not going to go help the bride?" Liam pointed toward the building to their left.

"Colton will get her to the reception. I just forgot something at home and need it before the reception." Danielle turned and stalked off, hoping he wouldn't see the tears forming in her eyes. She could hear her breathing increase as she pushed her steps forward, her stride lengthening with each one.

If anything, she was grateful for his bluntness. It would make it that much easier to avoid him from there on out—at least, when they weren't working on an article together.

*L*iam watched Danielle walk away, feeling something he'd never felt with Tawnee, his ex-girlfriend from New York. He'd dated his ex for nearly two years, and while he'd thought he was in love with her, he'd never gotten excited when she entered a room. Not like the flutters he'd felt when he saw Danielle reach the top of the hill and help Becca spread out her dress.

He was still intrigued by why she'd looked away when the bride and groom kissed. The action kept nagging at him. Maybe he'd just generalized all women world-wide when he thought they all loved romance and kissing. Danielle seemed like the exception to a lot of his past opinions. She might have bought romance books, but did she just skip over the kissing parts in those too?

After a few seconds of debate, he looked around and moved down the road to Canyon Street. One of the teenagers who lived down the block had volunteered to watch Cari during the ceremony. Liam was sure she wouldn't have made it through all of thirty minutes from beginning to end, even sitting by Mrs. McCready.

He picked Cari up, and they walked home, admiring the scenery along the way. They had at least around an hour before they'd have to be at the reception, mostly to let everyone get down from the pond and make sure the food was situated. Cari had been talking about nothing else for the past day than watching the bride and groom "cut a cake bigger than their faces."

"How was Tasha? Did you like playing with her?" Liam bent down to see her reaction and grinned as the girl took on a look that was much older than her six years. Her hand on her hip and her lips puckered out gave off a sassy impression, and Liam had to bite his upper lip to keep from laughing.

"She was really fun, and I think she gets me. We played with some of her old dolls, setting up a tea party, and when you came, the dolls were waiting for someone to rescue them from the crazy lady holding them hostage."

Liam's head jerked to look at his niece, hoping she was joking. "What do you mean? Was that something Tasha came up with?"

Cari shook her head. "No, I did."

Realization dawned as he remembered a section of a movie he'd been watching, a thriller, and he hadn't known she'd hidden by the side of the couch. He grimaced at what Tasha might think about what he exposed his niece to. "Cari, that's probably not the best thing to do. Next time, just play regular tea party, got it?" He stuck his thumb in the air.

She smiled, mimicking the action. "Okay. Did you have fun at the wedding?"

Liam's thoughts turned to the encounter with Danielle, and he nodded with a smile. "Yeah, it was good to see Colton get married."

"When are you going to get married, Uncle Liam? Wouldn't that make you happier?" Her comments made Liam stop and turn. Kneeling on the cement sidewalk, he placed his hands on her shoulders, drawing her attention to how serious he looked at the moment.

Searching her face, he asked, "What makes you think I'm not happy?"

"Abbey at school says people are only happy if they're married. I told her that's not true, that my mom is always happy with me. But maybe that's because she has someone. You don't. I just wondered if you wanted to be happy." She gave him a shy smile, watching his face for a reaction.

Pulling her into a hug, Liam held her for several seconds, realizing he probably needed it more than she did at that moment. When he pulled back, he brushed a piece of hair behind her ear. "Oh, Cari. I'm happy because I get to spend a lot of time with you."

"But you don't look happy when we're visiting my mom." Her tone of voice was sad, the sound whinier than he'd heard in a while.

Rubbing both hands over his face, Liam glanced at the sky, wishing he had the words to tell her everything that was going on inside him. "Your mom is very sick, and I have so many good memories with her that I hope she's here long enough to make great ones with you." He pointed to her chest, and Liam's throat closed up as his eyes filled with tears.

"Why won't she be around? I thought the doctors were going to do surgery and then she would just need to rest for a while. Where would she go if she's not around?"

Pulling her back against his chest, Liam wasn't sure how to answer those kinds of questions. "I'm not sure, Cari. We'll just see where we're at for the next few months."

She seemed to be okay with that because she moved out of his grasp and started skipping down the road. Liam watched as she walked so similarly to his sister that she could have passed for Kara thirty years ago.

His phone buzzed, and he pulled it out. Seeing the number of the hospital made his heart skip a beat. "Hello, this is Liam Pearson."

"Liam, this is Dr. Marcy. We got some tests back on your sister, and this is worse than we thought it would be. The cancer metastasized into several other organs, including her liver and one kidney. Can you come right away? We need to go over a game plan of how we want to take this on." She paused on the line. "I apologize that we didn't give you this news sooner. The specialist has been out until today and just looked at the exam results."

Liam's brain had to process all of that before he said, "Yes. I'll be right there."

After hanging up, he picked up Cari and threw her over his shoulder, jogging the last few houses to home.

"Why are you running? What's wrong with my mom?" Cari giggled and looked up at him with curious eyes as he finally put her down.

Shaking his head, Liam said, "The doctors just need to talk to us about some things they found on your mom's tests. I need to change, and then we'll drive over and see your mommy. How does that sound?"

Cari nodded, mumbling something about what she could take to her mother. As Liam thought about the conversation, he realized how important it was to keep the panic he felt inside him, not wanting to distress his niece. He could only imagine the outcomes now. They would be doing surgery on the tumors in her leg, but how had they not caught the ones in her kidney and liver until now? How could things change so quickly?

Liam raced downstairs after pulling on a comfortable pair of jeans and a maroon t-shirt, already feeling more comfortable than he had in the black suit he'd been wearing. He took the stairs two at a time and grabbed a small bag of cheese crackers for Cari to munch on during the drive. She'd need food since it was nearing dinner time, but Liam wanted to get to the hospital as soon as possible, hoping to get rid of the anxiety packing itself together tighter and tighter like a snowball.

Before putting the car into drive, Liam sent a text to Colton, knowing he probably wouldn't get it until later that evening.

It's Kara. I'm sorry about the speech.

He pulled out, trying to go a normal speed, when a text sounded. Pressing the button on his screen, the car read him the text as he weaved down the road leading down to the highway.

No worries. I'll make sure it gets taken care of.

In his mind, Liam said a prayer that everything would turn out. He just hoped it wasn't too late for his sister to recover from this.

*D*anielle was exhausted but happy for her best friend. Her eyes darted around the room, taking in the scene, and she smiled at the support Becca had after all the tragedies she'd suffered in her life. This town really was better off for knowing Rebecca Taylor, now Maxfield, but she had been shaped by each of them over the past several years as well.

"We need to get you up to the head table so we can have everyone settle in. We'll have Mayor Watkins say a few words in lieu of Becca's father, and then the best man and you will give your speeches." The wedding planner pulled her a little in the direction she wanted Danielle to go and then let go, flitting off to some other part of the reception hall.

As she looked around, Danielle took in the beauty of the room. The woman had done a great job overall, and it worked out better that the ceremony had been by the reservoir instead of in the rec hall so everything could be set up for the reception beforehand.

Danielle took her seat and looked down the small table. The mayor and his wife were sitting next to her on the side of the bride, with Tara and Carissa on Danielle's right. Colton's mother sat on the other side of him, beaming. But the spot next to her had been filled by Tanner, who'd made it to the reception. His cheeks looked a little flushed, but he was smiling about something Colton's mother said. Where was Liam?

After a quick search around the hall and not seeing him anywhere, it made her more curious. She shouldn't worry about him, shouldn't give him a second thought more than a writing partner for the newspaper, but she couldn't help but wonder what would pull him away from the wedding.

Leaning over to Mrs. Watkins, she whispered, "Where is Liam? Isn't he supposed to give a speech as well?"

Mrs. Watkins turned her head to look around the room and then looked over to Colton's side. "He's probably just running late, or had to get Cari."

Mayor Watkins stood, turning Mrs. Watkins's attention forward, and Danielle couldn't ask any more questions. Maybe something happened to Kara that had Liam and Cari heading to Grand Junction now.

Not that she was interested in him, because that wasn't the case. She'd pledged long ago not to let a relationship derail her life. But she couldn't help but smile as she remembered their bantering, something most people in Sage Creek didn't care for.

Sitting back in her seat, Danielle took a deep breath, feeling a hollowness sink into her chest. Maybe she needed to head back to LA, because she didn't feel the same kind of pressure there. Everyone just did their thing, focusing on work and playing on the weekends.

Soon enough, it was her turn to stand, and she tried to regroup her thoughts as she took the microphone.

"Thank you for your words, Tanner." She glanced over at him with a smile, not having heard any of his speech. She turned back to the crowd. "I just wanted to say I am so excited for the two of you," she said, looking at the bride and groom, "for the adventures you'll have over these next several decades and for your future. I've known Becca since the time we were in kindergarten, and we've been closer than honeycomb ever since. She's read some of my worst writing ever, and I've gladly accepted the random plants she's tried to grow in the backyard."

The crowd chuckled at that, and Danielle paused, her emotions sobering. "I know this means our lives are changing, for the better, and I wish you both many years of love." She raised her glass and took a sip as everyone else did the same.

Following dinner were the first dances, and she danced with Tanner, which didn't have the same electricity as when she was near Liam. With the cake cut, the bouquet toss went to Susie Jones, who looked more surprised than anyone since she wasn't dating anyone.

Once the couple headed out in Colton's truck, Danielle sighed. This day had been so much better than the one Becca was to share with Peter a few years ago. She'd never seen Becca happier.

Feeling the onset of another headache, Danielle slipped out of the rec hall and walked down the quiet streets. That was one good thing about a small town: when everyone was at an event, the streets were empty enough to enjoy in peace.

She walked aimlessly and found herself in front of the bookstore, peering into the dark rooms. A mental picture of the owner came into her mind, and her attraction to him grew as she thought of how he took care of his niece and that his wit rivaled her own.

Moving away from the glass, she tried to push any thoughts of Liam Pearson out of her brain. She just needed to focus on the article and her next cozy mystery and move on from there.

Escaping back into her mother's still house, she walked up to her room and pulled out her laptop. Nothing to squash thoughts about love like drafting her next cozy mystery.

CHAPTER 15

"I'm sorry, Mr. Pearson. It looks like the cancer has spread to her other organs. Our best chance is to surgically remove as many of the tumors as possible." Dr. Marcy pushed her glasses up higher on her nose, her face a mask trying to hide the sadness in her eyes.

Liam shifted his weight to the other foot, folding his arms against his chest. "And if you can't get them all?" His mind went immediately to Cari, and he turned, making sure she was okay in the room adjacent. She sat happily tapping away on his phone.

Dr. Marcy nodded as if she'd been waiting for this question. "We have a couple of options. The first is that we can try radiation and chemotherapy, but there isn't a guarantee those will work. The second is that we let her go home and she has maybe three to six weeks left."

Liam felt like he'd been hit by a car, the words slamming him in the chest and taking the oxygen with it. He took a step back, sinking into the chair. Turning to look through the window, he glanced in Cari's direction again, to find her singing and dancing to some song he couldn't hear.

Looking up at the doctor, he said, "But if we go through all the treatments, what are the outcomes for those?"

"Maybe another year."

"Maybe?" Liam said. The anger rose. "What about her daughter? Kara's got to live longer than that." Would he really lose his sister?

Sympathy spread over the doctor's features, and her voice came out softer this time. "I'm really sorry, Liam. I know how much she means to you, and I wish we had been able to find this sooner. But this type of cancer is resistant to most forms of treatment. There are some trials we could put her into and see how she does, but that will be something you need to discuss with her."

"Is she awake?" He'd convince her now to start the trial. Anything to keep her with him and Cari for a while longer.

"She woke up just a few minutes before you arrived. I'll check to find out if she's up to seeing you, but the sooner we make decisions in regards to her treatments, the better our chances are of prolonging some part of her life, even if we only add a few more weeks to it."

Liam stood and shook the doctor's hand, ready to take Cari to see her mother. A thought struck him as he moved to the door, and he turned around. "Are the treatments rough? I mean, will they make her sick?"

Dr. Marcy's face softened, and she nodded. "Usually sick days follow the treatments. The number of treatments and how close together they will be will determine whether she has any good days left."

Biting his bottom lip, he nodded. They both left the room, and Liam pasted a smile on his face before walking into the space next door. "Hey, Cari. Are you ready to see your mom?"

The girl's light brown hair fell into her face, and she moved it with her hand. "Is she awake?" Her eyes were wide beneath her glasses, and a big grin spread across her face as she waited for his answer.

"The doctor said she's going to go check on her. She must have known you were coming and wanted to be awake for it." Liam smiled, trying to mask the emotions of all the information he'd just been given.

When Kara received her diagnosis, Liam had just assumed that her mother-in-law in the next town over would be able to care for Cari, should anything happen. But as the weeks had gone on and Cari spent more and more time with him, he didn't know if he would be able to let go of her. And with the information he'd just received, he probably needed to plan to take care of her full time, or at least make arrangements to be in her life.

A nurse came for them, leading them through a long hallway and stopping before a door. "She's a little tired, but she was excited when I said you were here," the woman said, addressing Cari.

Her words made Cari bounce on her heels and clap her hands together. "Can I open the door?"

The nurse nodded, and Cari burst through. Liam waited in the hall for a few more seconds, not wanting to intrude on the mother-daughter moment.

As he crossed the threshold, he tried not to gasp as he saw his sister's face, so gaunt and pale. He'd seen her in person only a week earlier, but now she seemed like a different person. If he hadn't recognized her weak smile, he would've walked back out to check the name of the patient on the door. Lines pulled around her eyes as she listened to Cari talking a mile a minute, spilling all about everything that had happened since the last time they'd seen her.

Liam took a seat against the wall, knowing he'd have to talk about the options with his sister soon enough. None of them came with the guarantee he wanted.

He wouldn't be able to sit and watch his sister come home and slowly waste away. What would that do to Cari? But he also didn't want to see her go through any more pain or sickness. In all reality, that was the final conclusion. She would have to go through pain and sickness no matter what they did for her.

Rubbing his hands over his face, he took in a few breaths.

Cari had finished talking, and Kara was looking at him out of the corner of her eyes. "What's eating you?" she asked, her voice sounding like she hadn't spoken in years, cracking and soft.

"Life. Cari, why don't you take my tablet and go out to the nurses' station for a minute. I need to talk to your mom about a few things."

"I can't stay?" Cari turned to him with her big brown eyes, and as much as Liam wanted to give in and let her stay, he knew it would haunt the both of them forever if she started to have nightmares.

Kara moved her head a few inches and said, "Baby, just go out for a minute, and then you can come back in and tell me all about school. I love you."

"I love you too, Mommy. I hope you can come home soon. I miss you. Liam only makes mac and cheese and cereal."

"I made you pancakes yesterday, and the day before that." He tilted his head and gave her a side-eye, causing Cari to grin.

Kara tried to laugh, which turned into a cough, the movement shaking her whole body. Liam rushed forward with his hands out, ready to help with whatever was needed. When the coughing fit ended, she said, "We should probably teach him how to cook something else, huh? And do it without burning the house down."

Liam smiled at that, knowing full well what she meant.

"That was one time, and nothing burned down. The wall was just black behind the stove." It had happened when they were teenagers and their parents had gone out for dinner. Liam had tried to cook some kind of meat but forgot about it, and the whole thing caught on fire.

Cari looked interested in that, but Liam gently guided her to the door and then watched as she walked over to a chair by the nurses' station. Shutting the door with a click, the sound made it seem like he was closing one part of his life, even though he wasn't quite ready for that chapter to be done.

"You look like someone took your puppy. What is it?"

"Doctor Marcy said the cancer has already spread throughout the rest of your body."

Kara nodded. "I figured that's what happened. I haven't felt much different after the surgery than I did before."

Liam looked at her, wondering how to tell her which way to choose. "We have a few options. We can do treatments, put you into some trials, or have you come home where chances are high that you'll only have a couple of weeks."

Kara was silent, and her gaze turned to the ceiling. The machines beeping in the background told him she was stable for the minute. Things were so quiet, and he wasn't sure whether he should keep talking or not. After a bit, he opened his mouth to speak, but Kara beat him to it.

"Let's do the treatments. If I don't respond, we'll do the trials."

Liam moved the chair next to her bed and took her hand in his. "The doctor said you might not have many good days, depending on how many treatments you have."

A tear rolled down her cheek, and Liam did the best he could to keep his own tears at bay. She gave him a sad smile. "That little girl out there is worth it. If I can just have a little more time with her, create a few more memories for her to remember me by when I'm gone, then I'll fight through any of the bad days I have to."

Liam couldn't hold back his emotions anymore and fought to see through the tears in his eyes. "I can't lose you too." A mound had formed in his throat, and he tried to swallow past it, causing the constriction to tighten even more.

Kara squeezed his hand. "You're strong. I hate to place this burden on you, but will you be her guardian when I'm gone? I love Sarah, but she's older and doesn't have the physical strength to take care of an energetic six-year-old."

"I'll do it. Of course, I'll take care of her."

Biting her upper lip, Kara nodded, more tears streaming down her face. "You need to find yourself a girl."

Liam laughed and wiped at his cheeks. "That was a change in subject."

"No, it wasn't. She'll be special, whoever she is, and hopefully she'll love my little girl the way you always have." Kara took in a deep breath, looking like talking had worn her out. "It's better to love than not take the leap, Liam. If you're not going to do it for yourself, do it for me. I'll never regret marrying Cory, even if I'd known I'd lose him after all we went through when we lost Mom and Dad."

Patting her hand, Liam said, "Rest. I'll talk to the doctors and see what arrangements can be made. You're sure, then? You want to go through with the treatments?"

She smiled. "Absolutely. If those don't work, we'll move on to the trials."

"Okay. We'll get a hotel and come see you in the morning." Liam winked at her before entering the hall and closing the door.

Walking up to the nurse at the desk, he said, "My sister wants to go forward with whatever treatments the doctors recommend."

The nurse gave him a sad smile. She moved to get some papers and then said, "I'll let the doctor know."

Liam nodded and strode over to sit by Cari. "Hey, girl. Let's go get a hotel. We'll buy you a swimsuit so you can swim, and we'll come see your mom tomorrow."

As Cari placed her hand in his, he knew things were changing, and Kara's words echoed in his mind. Find a girl. He would've been lucky to find one willing to consider him *without* Cari in the picture. He'd just have to trust that things would work out, or that if the next steps didn't work out, maybe one of the trials would save his sister.

He reflected on his time with Tawnee, the real reason he hadn't pursued anyone else in the past six months. She'd been a pathological liar, and when it all came to light, he was surprised he'd lasted as long as he had in the relationship. Would he be able to open himself up to someone else?

Danielle's face popped into his mind, and his curiosity grew. She didn't seem like the type to be in a long-term relationship. But then again, he wouldn't mind getting to know her better.

CHAPTER 16

Danielle had gotten a text from Liam saying he wouldn't make it Sunday afternoon. They'd rescheduled for Monday, but when he didn't come at the designated time or another hour after, she wondered if she'd gotten the time wrong. Had he counted their agreement on a topic as canceling their meeting?

Pulling out her phone, she scrolled through the short list of messages they'd sent back and forth, wondering why he hadn't at least given her a heads-up about not coming. Maybe he'd had to take care of Cari or some emergency happened with his sister. He'd mentioned something about hoping Kara would be able to come home on Sunday.

Danielle paid her tab at the diner and walked along Main Street, seeing the darkness inside the bookstore. Since she'd been here nearly a week, the only time she'd seen the store black was on Sunday, which wasn't a rare occurrence in town. The only place usually open then was the gas station.

Taking her laptop to the park, she sat on one of the benches, trying to focus on the outline for the next MK Malone book. She'd felt the block in her brain for the last twenty-four hours, and she hoped it wouldn't stay long. As far as steady work was going, she kept striking out with every station and larger newspaper she'd applied for, and the need to do something other than sit at home or roam the streets of Sage Creek was eating at her.

She plugged in her wireless connection and pulled up her stats for her mystery books. She was surprised at the spike in sales of her books since she'd come back to Sage Creek last Tuesday. It was almost laughable that something she'd written and hadn't promoted hardly at all was actually making some money.

At least that was encouraging, since she felt like everything in her life was unraveling. Opening her Word document, she reread the last few lines she'd written from the day before, honing in on where she would take her heroine next.

She didn't know how long she'd been there, but the bench moved slightly as someone sat next to her. Looking over, she saw it was Liam, and a wave of relief rolled over her. She'd never really been worried about anyone, but with all the assumptions she'd made, it was good to see him there uninjured.

"I'm sorry to startle you. You looked like you were really focused on whatever you're working on." Liam smiled and leaned over, trying to focus on the words.

Danielle shut the laptop with a loud click, hoping he hadn't recognized anything. She still didn't want anyone to know about her alternate identity, especially Liam. She'd never felt comfortable discussing her writing with anyone outside of Becca, because many people didn't get it. And now that things were going well with the three books she already had out, she didn't want to jinx it or chance anyone in town figuring out who she was.

"It's good to see you're alive and not some phantom." She

smiled, hoping her raised eyebrow would convey the questions probing her mind.

"I promise I don't live in an opera house." The corner of his mouth turned up.

Danielle had to roll in her lips to keep from sighing. The brightness of his baby blues drew her in, and given the opportunity, she could probably stare at them for longer than comfortable. Why was she so attracted to him? She hadn't felt like this in, well, ever. It was as if she was turning into some bright-eyed school girl with a crush. Something she'd worked diligently to control over the years.

She ran her hands through her long hair, pulling out some tangles in the process. It was her attempt to make the questions she said next casual, but he didn't seem to notice. "So, what happened to you? Tanner had to give the best man speech, and I'm a little ashamed to say I was curious about what you would've said in yours."

Liam chuckled, the sound deep and rough, causing Danielle to do the same. "You want to know what I would've said? Well, I can tell you right now." He positioned a hand just below his mouth to look like he was holding a microphone. "Welcome, everyone. I've known Colton since May. He took me in as I adjusted to life in a small town, and although we've only known each other for a few months, he's one of those people you can count on to be there for you. I'm excited for you both, and I wish you all the happiness in the world." He moved his hand out to the side and tilted his head forward in a bow.

"That was pretty good. It seems you, Colton, and Tanner are like the three musketeers."

"Well, I've always wanted to be in a sword fight, so maybe there's something to your theory."

Danielle wasn't sure what her expression looked like, but Liam's loud laugh caused her to relax a bit.

Liam spoke again. "What about you and Becca? I'm assuming you grew up together here."

"Yep. I met her in Kindergarten, actually."

"Wow. That's a long time. Was it hard being in the same town forever?"

Danielle thought about that for a moment. "No, I think the only reason I survived here was because of Becca. She was my constant when no one really understood me." She looked at him with her eyes narrowed. "I thought you were going to miss our meeting today. Did you have something come up?"

Liam nodded and looked remorseful. "Yeah, I was driving back from Grand Junction and just got here. Sorry, I probably should have thought to text you earlier."

A warm feeling came over Danielle, and she waved it off. "Is everything okay with your sister?"

His mouth dropped into a frown. "It's…we got some bad news. But we have a few options, and I hope they work to get rid of the cancer. Or at least give her more time."

Tears sprang to her eyes, and Danielle reached over, wrapping her arms around him. She tried to tell herself it was only to comfort him, but the closeness seemed like static electricity that flowed throughout her body. He returned the hug, and she breathed in, the same woodsy scent from before filling her nose.

She finally pulled away, wiping at the stray tear escaping down her face. "I'm, uh, sorry. It just reminded me of the pain Becca went through when she lost her family. I hope the treatments work too. Kara is such a great person, and I hope she can be here for many more years. How's Cari taking all of it?"

Liam gave her a half-smile, swallowing hard. "Thank you. Cari doesn't understand most of it, and I'm not sure what to tell her until they figure out what's working and what's not." He looked down at his hands for a minute as if they were useless to what he was going through right now. He looked up at her again with a broader smile. "Anyway, since I arrived late, we should probably decide what we want to write about. Do you still want to go with what society thinks we should be doing at our age?"

"I think that would be good. We should probably pick a few other ages, just to hit different people in town so it's not so pointed to the thirty-year-olds."

Laughing, Liam said, "I'm not thirty. And you aren't either."

"No, but I thought you might be. Let me guess. Twenty-seven?"

Red tinged his cheeks just enough to make her smile. "Close. Twenty-eight. And you said you are twenty years younger than your mom, who is forty-seven. So you're twenty-seven, like Becca?" His one eyebrow rose.

Danielle laughed and nodded. "Well, I'm sure you get the 'Why aren't you married yet? You're such a nice young man; you should be married already' speech. I know I've gotten it several times just since Tuesday." She rolled her eyes, and Liam chuckled. "Not the young man part, but you get the idea."

"Yes, that seems to be the first conclusion people jump to. I usually just smile and nod, trying to tell them I really don't need a blind date with their sister's best friend's aunt's daughter who's about my age and still single." He leaned forward, a hint of a smile on his lips. "I have to avoid the beginning of the book groups because they're always trying to set me up. I don't have control over the end because I want people to buy stuff from the store."

As much as Danielle tried to hold it in, a loud laugh came barreling out, and she leaned over, unable to stop.

With a small smile, Liam said, "Go ahead and laugh. I've lost count how many times that's happened. Blind dates—"

"Are the worst! And it feels like that's what everyone does here in Sage Creek. The older people are amazing, but they're bored, and they love to watch a couple get together. I'm sure some of them were out with popcorn, watching as Becca and Colton started dating." Danielle thought about it and laughed softer this time.

"You're right about that." There had been so many people invested in the newlyweds' relationship, especially after Becca's previous fiancé didn't show up for the day of the wedding.

Liam cleared his throat. "I've been able to avoid some of the older people in that regard, thank goodness. I'm just going along, trying to make things fun in the town, but don't send me a number for a blind date."

Danielle raised a hand. "No worries there. As long as you don't have someone to line me up with either, I think we'll be just fine."

Liam raised both hands. "Nope, all of my guy friends are married or out of the country, so I think you're safe. Except for Tanner, but I think he has eyes on someone else in town."

That sparked the intrigue of her journalist side. "Do tell."

"I think he has a thing for the local bridal store owner." His smile was conspiratorial, and he nodded a few times as if that would convince Danielle of the truth of it.

Tanner liked Susie? That would be an interesting matchup. Then again, it would be like the quarterback and the head cheerleader dating, although Tanner was significantly more shy than the average jock.

Liam and Danielle sat on the bench, the silence between them peaceful, and she looked over once, admiring his profile. After a bit, she said, "Don't you have to open your bookstore?"

As if that spurred him into action, Liam jumped up. "Yes, actually. Sorry, I've got to go."

Danielle stood as well. "How about if I walk with you? I'm done with the park for today anyway."

They started walking on the sidewalk back to Main Street, and Liam pointed to her laptop. "What were you working on?"

After some hesitation, Danielle said, "Just some thoughts. I've toyed around with the idea of writing books. But that could just be a pipe dream." The lie hurt, but she still wasn't ready to tell anyone. As much as she was used to the spotlight for the news, she kind of enjoyed the anonymity of hearing what people thought of her books without them knowing they were written by her.

Liam stuffed his hands into his pockets, something Danielle liked as it emphasized the muscles in his upper arms. "I don't know. I've read that MK Malone is a self-published author. There are a lot of opportunities these days. Maybe you could be the next rising star." He smiled at her, his white teeth gleaming in the sunlight.

Danielle nodded. "Maybe. I have to write the book first." Plotting was taking longer than it had the times before, and she worried the fourth book wouldn't be as good as the earlier ones.

"Well, I have a minor in English, so if you ever need to bounce ideas or someone to read your stuff, let me know."

A thrill shot up her back, and she smiled at him. "Thank you. You're probably the only person to ever offer besides Becca. Which isn't saying much because writing is not her forte."

"I've read a few of your articles, and I think you have a talent with words. We could be reading one of your books this time next week."

Danielle held out her hand. "Hold on there, city boy. I'd

be lucky to have the first draft written by next week. Editing, proofing, cover design…that all takes time."

Liam chuckled, the sound making her think of smooth chocolate for some reason. A few seconds later, his face sobered. "I've been thinking about emailing MK Malone to see if he or she would come talk at the bookstore sometime. If it happens, I'll make sure you have some time to pick his or her brain."

Danielle stopped a minute, her brain in overdrive. She felt her heart soften toward this gorgeous man, that he would do something like that for her when they were little more than acquaintances. But her mind then registered that he would be emailing *her* to come and speak to Sage Creek. What mess had she gotten herself into?

He turned and waited for her to catch up.

She'd have to put the kibosh on that plan as soon as possible.

CHAPTER 17

*L*iam smiled as he switched books from one shelf to another Tuesday morning. It was usually the slowest day of the week, and he had a system for rotating out the books depending on season, month, or event. The rotation helped the frequent shoppers to see something new. Impulse buys moved books.

Thoughts about Danielle floated through his mind. He liked her spunk and how she was so forward about her feelings on just about everything. The fact that she was thinking about writing a book was admirable. He'd always thought about writing books but had been too busy in New York.

Now, taking care of Cari and Kara the past several months, he felt like all of his thoughts about fantasy worlds had been frozen, the creativity not coming to him when he actually sat down to write. It was one of the reasons he'd volunteered to copyedit and then write for the newspaper, in the hopes that it would help spark some creativity after writing about opinions and facts.

He needed to get started on his article as he only had a couple of days left to write and edit his thoughts, which usually needed more time to flesh out. Maybe a deadline would be the key to pushing his brain to the limit. They'd be driving back and forth to Grand Junction after school every day when they could, hoping to spend as much time as they could with Kara, so his time would be limited. The treatments made her sick, but she was able to interact with them for about an hour before she needed rest.

The bell on the door rang, and he looked over one of the shelves and saw Danielle walk into the store.

"Are you looking for another stack of books? Because I think you'll like that section over there." He grinned at her as he walked out from behind the shelves. "I just moved the mystery section."

She smiled and nodded. "Thank you. I actually just finished the last book in my stack around two this morning and figured I'd come in for some more entertainment. I wrote a few chapters last night for my book, so I'm on a roll." Her grin looked giddy, like it was some miracle she'd done that much.

Leaning an arm on the shelf, Liam said, "Do you read a lot to get inspiration?"

"I guess so. I haven't really thought about it like that." She turned her gaze to the bookshelf next to her, her fingers moving over the spines of the books there.

With her light brown hair falling in waves over her shoulder, Liam found her simple beauty alluring. Tawnee had barely ever let him see her without makeup on and her hair done, and while he'd seen video clips of Danielle reporting the news, she didn't look like a completely different person in real life.

But was that attraction enough to take away his fears of being in a relationship again? Not that Danielle gave off the vibe she was willing to date anyone. Colton had said something about a ban against dating, and he suddenly wanted to know what would lead her to that. An ex-boyfriend, maybe?

Realizing he was staring, Liam said, "Let me know if you need something." He turned and ducked behind the shelf, doing his best to focus on the titles he'd already moved.

"Actually, I was curious if you've already emailed MK Malone."

Popping his head back around the shelf, he said, "No. I haven't quite figured out how to word it, or what we could offer in exchange for a visit. I know some of the bigger authors have a dollar amount attached to speaking arrangements, but I haven't read about anything for him. Our small bookstore wouldn't be able to afford a large sum for one event, but if it were a reasonable request, I'd find a way to make it happen."

"Maybe you should wait a bit. I'm sure he's probably working on his next book." She paused a moment before saying, "Wait. How did you know the author is a guy anyway? I've had trouble finding anything about him."

Liam shrugged. "I think I heard one of the ladies in your book club talking about the author as a guy, so I just assumed they knew something I didn't." He gave her a half-smile, and her face softened. "Why do you think I should wait? I think right now would be a great time since a lot of the town has read the three books that are out."

She looked hesitant about something and then said, "I don't know. It's up to you. Who knows if he'd have time to come here?" Something about the way she broached this topic made Liam suspicious, but he wasn't sure what it was that felt off.

"I'll let you know when I contact him. I've had a lot going on here, but it will be a treat for the people in town. The trilogy has been a good seller here, and it's been a challenge to come up with books I can stock as a supplement until the next one comes out."

Danielle tilted her head to the side a bit. "I never really considered all that goes into a bookstore. I guess I just thought of it as a place with a lot of books. But rotating where they're positioned, thinking about the ones that would be good for certain interests and personalities, even having the knowledge of so many books to be able to refer people to the books they need…that's impressive."

Liam's chest swelled with pride. "Why, thank you. My mother loved books. I think she'd be proud that we worked to make it happen."

"You and Kara?"

A stab of guilt filled him as he said, "Yes."

"What happened to your parents?"

"My dad passed away eight years ago. They diagnosed him with a brain tumor, and three months later, my mother passed away. She'd had muscular sclerosis since I was young."

Danielle's hand flew to her mouth, and her eyes went wide. The people who knew the family's background usually reacted the same. Two people with cancer and one with an autoimmune disease sounded like a curse. But his parents had been older and had accepted it after a longer life. Kara just needed that chance.

"I'm so sorry. I had no idea." She shook her head.

Liam moved forward, placing a hand hesitantly on her shoulder. "They never lived here, so you wouldn't have known. It's fine." After a breath, he asked, "What happened with your father? I've only ever heard people talk about Mrs. Holloway."

With a quick shrug, she said, "It's the classic story of the husband hitting a mid-life crisis and deciding he didn't want to be married anymore. I barely remember him."

The methodical tone of her voice and the mask she wore

hid feelings that had probably built over the years. That could be the reason she was often snarky and sarcastic, trying to hide the hurt and pain from years of whatever had happened to her.

"I'm sorry. I shouldn't have asked."

Danielle's face was somber, but she said, "Like you said, you couldn't have known. Not many people talk about it here, which is surprising in a small town. It's old news, and most people like my mother too much to speak badly about her. She's so sweet. Sometimes I wonder if I actually am her daughter." Again, the laugh sounded off, and Liam wondered if there was a part of her that believed it.

"Well, you're several inches taller than her, but other than that, you could pass as siblings."

She raised her eyebrow, and Liam felt himself backpedaling. "I mean that in a good way, you know, like you are a younger version of her if she were a really, like, a lot older sister and—"

"Liam."

"Huh?"

"Stop. You're fine. My mother would take that as a compliment." Danielle turned back to the books, and Liam was caught in the middle of the bookstore, wondering whether he should go back to work or continue the conversation.

"Let me know when you're ready to check out."

Moving back to his shelf, he peeked over, studying her from a safe distance. There were so many facets to her personality, and he felt like each time he talked with her, another one appeared. She could be blunt and sarcastic, but she also had a more sensitive side.

Then again, there was the fact that he'd just stumbled over every word that came out of his mouth. He had been an investment banker and had to talk to people all the time. But over the last few days, he'd been doing word gymnastics when he was around Danielle.

Maybe he needed a nap and a break from town. With Kara starting her first treatment on Thursday, he planned to head to Grand Junction, taking Cari out of school on Friday and making a weekend out of it. If things went well, he hoped to have his sister back home in the next few weeks, hopefully with a better overall outlook. He could dream that she'd be cured, but sooner or later he'd have to face the facts that he was going to lose yet another family member.

The article came to mind, and he knew he'd need to work on it throughout the evening. He didn't want to turn in a late post for his first try, and he could only imagine the smirk on Danielle's face if he did so.

His interest in Danielle could only go that far. His heart could only take so much, and losing his sister was going to pull it to pieces already.

CHAPTER 18

*D*anielle finished up her article on Thursday with a couple of minutes to spare until the deadline. She'd always been like that, working up to the last minute, usually because she'd procrastinated it until then. The familiar rush of excitement coursed through her when she sent it off to Clyde and wondered how it would look next to Liam's article.

Their conversation the other day at the bookstore still made her laugh and almost cry at the same time. It was so sad that his parents had both died, even though from different causes, and she couldn't imagine what that would be like. She was grateful to still have her mother around. It would've been hard without her there as a constant in her life, even when Danielle felt like everything she'd worked for was now in a pile of rubble.

If someone had told her the one bright spot of coming back here would be the handsome bookstore owner, she'd have laughed in their face. She tried to fight it, but she found herself looking for him when she went places, and his knowledge of books was astounding and made her painfully curious about him. As much as she'd worked to guard her heart against men in general, many of whom would abandon their women like her father, she found herself feeling more and more interested in Liam.

After pulling up the document for her latest MK Malone book, she stared at the screen for several minutes, trying to work out the plot points in her mind. The hardest part about cozy mysteries was hiding the killer so the reader wouldn't see it coming. She often worked backward, figuring out who the criminal was and then piling on the layers of doubt and distracting the main character with several red herrings. It was a challenge within itself, and when she got it to all line up perfectly, a rush of adrenaline would pour through her.

All she needed for this story were a few more elements and another twenty thousand words, and the story would be ready for her editor. She'd never met Tina in person, but the woman understood where Danielle was going with the story for the most part and would polish some of her rushed ideas, helping her connect the dots on plot points Danielle had forgotten to finish out.

The great thing about publishing was that everything could be done through online communication. Editor, proofer, cover. Her amazing cover designer took her ideas and created a cover that made Danielle smile and got people interested in the book, which was half the battle.

For a girl who'd loved the spotlight when it came to journalism through the newspaper and the occasional television appearance, she was afraid that if people knew she'd written these books, her world would change forever. That it would be ripped away just as journalism had.

Danielle's phone buzzed. *Just finished my article. Talk about race to the finish.*

She smiled as she read Liam's text, trying to come up with a response.

I took you for someone who finished the assignment the first day you got it. This surprises me, Pearson.

She pressed send, staring at her phone as she waited for a reply. It came a few minutes later, when she'd given up and gone back to staring at her few typed words.

I'm a box of wonders. Just wait.

anielle spent a few hours Tuesday morning typing and deleting the words on her laptop, not happy with how the story was turning out. She hadn't made much progress, even throughout the weekend, and realized she needed air and a change of scenery. She wished her mother wasn't at the store and could go with her and help her think of scenarios. Hypothetical ones, she'd tell her.

With Becca and Colton still on their honeymoon, she thought of Liam and wondered if he'd be up for a brainstorming session. Pulling out her phone, she saw it was still early, meaning he'd be at the bookstore. Her feet walked as her mind lagged behind, trying to come up with something that would wow her readers once the book was finished.

"Danielle!" a voice called as she made it to Main Street. "Danielle! Over here!"

Turning her head several times, Danielle finally spotted Mrs. Watkins sitting on a bench across the street. Next to her was Sharon Crestview, and Danielle wished she hadn't decided to leave her house. Sharon would be the death of her if she didn't keep focused.

Trudging over to the women, it wasn't until she was a few feet away that she noticed the Sunday newspaper folded between them. She'd been so focused on writing her book that she hadn't taken the time to read it yet.

Sharon opened it and folded the front page back, revealing the editorial section. "This is quite an interesting article," she said, her voice sugary sweet.

"I thought it was refreshing, Sharon. It's much better than Nolan's boring tales of the birds and their mating and migration habits." Mrs. Watkins winked at Danielle. "I especially loved the part where you talk about expectations of us older folks. So many people think once you're retired, you sit in a chair all day and knit if you're a woman. Thank you for saying we can still participate in society at my age."

Danielle wasn't sure what to say and chuckled. "No problem." She edged closer, realizing her curiosity over Liam's part of the article took over. "Do you mind if I take a look at that for a moment? I didn't get to see the opposing article."

Sharon handed the paper over, and Danielle took it, sitting where Mrs. Watkins had sat before scooting over for her. She read, the world around her nonexistent.

Expectations. They're the things we hope for, wait for, dream of. Sometimes they're the things we're scared of and wish could just disappear from our lives. As we turn sixteen, we're expected to want to drive a car, and then everyone fears for their lives as we barrel down the road, trying to learn how to control this new freedom we have. At twenty-five, either we're supposed to be making millions, or at the beginning of a master's degree, on our way to greatness and halfway up the ladder we're expected to climb in our lifetime.

If we haven't married by the time we're twenty-eight, with plans for kids two years later, something must be wrong with us. And just like a cough, everyone has a suggestion as to how to get rid of it, usually bringing over the cure they think will help.

At forty, we should be settled into a career that we love, or that we grin and bear through every day because we know it will all be for the best for our growing family. We need money, and it's too late to branch out and start something new. As a male, we feel the pressure to succeed to such heights, all while keeping in every worry and emotion because those around us won't understand that venting doesn't mean the end of the world.

At sixty-five, we are supposed to relax and retire, hoping we've made enough to survive until we pass away. We wake up every day, wondering whether it will be us or our spouse who departs this life first and hoping the grandchildren come to visit.

Danielle looked up at the women next to her, their soft chatting sounding a lot like a couple of hens. If Liam had been smart, he would have mentioned that the women should go first so the man could have some peace for a bit before he passed on.

She looked down again, continuing to read the rest.

But all these are just expectations. Assumptions of what another person deems a benchmark of success. The problem, men, is that we need to be working toward what makes us happy. Now, I'm not saying you should skip out on your relationship or decide to take up thievery. Our goal in life should be something that makes us happy.

If we need a bit longer to learn how to drive, there's nothing wrong with that, although the freedom is amazing, even if it's your mother sending you to the grocery store five times that day. If you don't like the job at forty that you chose at twenty-five, find a way to change it. Whether it's taking a leap and starting the company you've always wanted or just walking away from the high-paying job because it only gives you health problems and stress, find a way to make it work.

If you're not married yet and you're thirty, forty, fifty, or beyond, it's not the end of the world. You'll figure it out, and either someone will come into your life that you need at that precise moment, or you'll find a way to make yourself happy without depending on the actions of someone else to do so.

At forty and above, you're allowed to decide when you retire and what those activities should be. If you have a spouse, they deserve a chance to help decide what those activities are, but if you do things together, your relationship is that much stronger. Because after the kids are gone, all you have left is each other.

I guess what I'm saying is, whatever you're doing and however experiences have changed and molded your life, roll with it. Move forward, strive to be the best person you can be, and no matter what has happened in your life, it will work out well. You'll be the person you need to be for neighbors and for your family.

Danielle looked up again and found herself a bit teary as she thought about the simplicity of his words. He hadn't tried to dance around the issue but had stated the problems and given permission to be happy no matter what stage of life.

"It's amazing, isn't it?" Sharon said, her voice soft.

Danielle thought she saw the older woman blink back tears, and she realized how little she really knew of Sharon's background. The woman had lost her husband a few years before, and while Danielle didn't pretend to know how that felt, she could imagine it would be difficult all year round with all the little dates that popped up, whether it was the anniversary of his passing, of their wedding, or even just a smell or a song that brought the reminder.

With a quick nod, Danielle folded the paper again and handed it back. Standing, she brushed off her backside, trying to occupy her thoughts. "Yes, that was an incredible piece."

Mrs. Watkins leaned forward and touched Danielle's forearm. "Yours was beautiful too, my dear. The pieces together make for a great read."

Danielle gave her a smile and then said, "I need to get some things done, so I'll catch the two of you later."

Moving away before they could object, she found herself outside the bookstore, looking in. She didn't have an excuse as to why she was there this time, but she felt confident she didn't really need one. She just wanted to praise him on the article.

Opening the door, she saw Liam behind the desk, and when they locked eyes, his smile made her insides flip. "Back so soon? I don't think I have many other new books in stock for you, in the mystery section at least."

Danielle shook her head, moving over to lean on the desk. "I'm not here for that. I just wanted to tell you I read your part of the article, and you did an amazing job with it."

Liam moved forward, bringing with him a fresh sea smell. "I thought yours was well-written also."

With a scoff, Danielle said, "I'm not so sure. There were a lot of parts I had a hard time writing. But I liked the overall theme you had that being yourself is enough."

The blank look on his face made Danielle squirm.

"I don't remember writing that." His eyebrow rose, and he stared into her eyes, waiting for an explanation.

"I didn't mean you wrote that exactly, but that was the overall impression I got from it."

Liam opened his mouth wide in an O shape. "Should we talk about the topic for the next one?"

"Clyde hasn't even gotten feedback from this one today. Let's wait until we hear from him to think we can toot our own horns."

"You're right," Liam said with a grin. "How's your book-writing going, by the way? I keep waiting to hear from you, saying you need someone to read through it, but all I get is a silent phone." The look on his face said he was half joking, and Danielle turned on the charm.

"I wasn't sure you were serious about that. I'm not at that point yet, but when I am, I'll let you know."

Raising an eyebrow, he asked, "Really? Because whenever we talk about your writing, you get a little weird and try to avoid everything about it."

Why was it that he was the one who could read her like a book? Sure, that sounded cliché since he was the bookstore owner, but he was so perceptive about the small things that most people overlooked.

Danielle took her pointer finger and waved it in an X across her heart. "I cross my heart and hope to die that I will let you know as soon as I have something worth looking at."

Liam's smile spread so wide that his eyes seemed to get lost, turning into slits. "I'll take it."

Danielle moved a few steps toward the door. "Well, I'd better get back to it. Again, good article, and I'll see you around."

"What about dinner tomorrow night?"

She paused, frozen in place. Unsure what to say, she turned, the words stuck in her mouth at the unexpected request. Having him ask her on a date was something she'd subconsciously wanted but had never imagined would happen in real life.

"Are you asking me on a date?" she asked, the wobble in her voice causing her to shift nervously.

His blue eyes bored into hers. "Only if you want it to be. Otherwise, it can be colleagues talking about similar interests." The one corner of his mouth hitched up again, and Danielle couldn't break her gaze away from his lips, wondering what they would feel like to kiss.

"I think I can arrange that. What time?"

"How about four thirty? Wednesdays are slow anyway, and I can close up early and come get you."

She nodded. "What should I wear?"

He smiled again. "Whatever you want. After how busy things have been, I'm thinking we can do something relaxed where we can just talk and get to know each other better."

She gave him a quick nod and pushed the door open, hearing the bells ring above her. Stumbling out onto the sidewalk, she made her way back home. The walk passed quickly, and Danielle didn't notice much of anything going on around her, her thoughts moving around the date the next day.

Entering the house, she grabbed a cup from the cabinet in the kitchen and filled it with water, realizing how thirsty she was just now.

"Long day?" her mother asked from behind her, causing Danielle to jump. Water trickled down her face and onto the old t-shirt she'd been wearing since five that morning. Looking down, she groaned. Why hadn't she thought to change what she had on before going out in public? People were probably talking about how she was letting herself go.

"Yes. I'm working on a few writing projects, and I can't quite get the details right."

The surprise on her mother's face made Danielle feel guilty that she'd kept so many secrets from her. But she still wasn't ready to reveal who MK Malone was, so she kept her mouth shut.

"What projects?" her mother asked, putting down her purse and taking off her name tag. She looked like she'd been through the wringer herself.

Danielle walked to the fridge, trying to see if there was something easy she could make for dinner to give her mom a break from cooking.

"Just thought about writing a book." Danielle's enthusiasm helped her smile wide, which was something she hadn't done with regard to her writing dreams in so long that it felt forced.

"I take it you don't have any other job offers at the moment?" Her mother leaned against the cabinet.

Danielle took a breath, readying herself for whatever argument was on the brink. "Mom, you know I love to write. Why is it you think that's not good enough for me to do as a career?"

Her mother reached out and placed her palm on Danielle's cheek. "Dear, I just want you to be happy. And I guess my idea of your happiness was the dream of you with a stable job. If that's not what you want, then I get it. I just don't want you wasting your life away when things don't change or you put in a lot of effort for peanuts. Like the newspaper."

"What are you talking about? I love to write, and this weekend's article was one of my favorite pieces thus far. I know it's hard to imagine when I'm not interacting with people all day every day, but it's still work."

With a look of dismay, her mother moved past her and pulled a package of hamburger meat from the fridge.

"Mom, I'm not trying to down your job. I know how much the grocery store has helped us through the years and while I was growing up. I just wanted something different for my life."

"I get that, Danielle, but when is enough, enough? When will you realize that this is your life and you need to live it? That you need to contribute to the world around you?"

Danielle spotted the MK Malone book from the book club sitting on the countertop. She moved toward it and pick it up. She closed the distance between her and her mother, waving the book in front of her mother's face. "What do you think about this, Mom? Does this writer contribute to society?"

Her mother seemed to think about it. "I guess. It's enter-tainment, and that can bring in money."

Slapping it onto the counter, Danielle said, "Well, you're looking at the author of this book, Mom."

"What? Don't do this right now, Dani. I'm not in the mood to battle it out with you. And there's no need to lie about it." She bent to pull a pan from underneath the oven and set it on the cooktop.

"No, Mom. I wrote this and the other two books. I've been working on book number four for the past two weeks, more since I've been here. I wrote the character of Holly Frontier, the woman who's always stumbling onto a murder scene. I based her off of you, Mom." She raised her hands quickly. "Not the way she's always finding body parts, but the quiet strength she has, the ability to reason things out in her head before even speaking."

"You really are MK Malone? But I showed you the book the other day, and you looked like you'd never heard of it before."

Danielle chuckled. "I wasn't expecting to ever see a physical copy of it in the hands of someone I know, let alone my own mother. It threw me for a moment, and then I was curious and wanted to know what the ladies would say."

Her mother frowned, indecision on her face.

Walking over to her laptop on the counter, Danielle sighed and opened it. Searching for the documents, she pulled up the folders she'd created for each of the books, every note and rough draft she'd been through all tucked neatly inside them. She pointed to the folders, and her mother's mouth dropped open. She kept looking between the computer screen and Danielle's face.

Danielle pulled up the website where her books were sold, showing her mother the results of her books thus far. "This is what I've made on these books. It's not millions, but it can support a modest lifestyle right now. And if I figure out the whole ads aspect of marketing, I might be able to up those amounts by significant margins."

Her mother's mouth went slack, looking as though she'd been punched. "You really wrote all those books? When did you have time to do all this?"

Danielle smirked. "I traveled a lot, Mom. I wrote between assignments and on my way to places. Until I saw the book at your book club, I had been too scared to check to see how they were doing."

"And?"

"And they're selling even outside of Sage Creek, which, to me, is saying something." She clicked a tab on the dashboard and scrolled down, revealing the countries where the books were being bought.

A smile crossed her mother's face, followed closely by a frown. "I'm so sorry, Dani. I know I haven't always been the most encouraging when it came to writing. But it seems you've proven me wrong once again."

Danielle moved forward and wrapped her arms around her mother. "It's fine. I just had to keep going, and I still have to. If I can make it with writing these books, I can stay here for a while longer. Just, please don't tell anyone yet."

They pulled apart, and her mother's eyes studied her face. "Are you sure that's what you want? I know you wanted to get out of this town as soon as you graduated high school."

"I can't say I won't have times when I get bit by the travel bug, but I'm learning to love some aspects of Sage Creek."

"I just hope you know I love you, and that I'm here to support you, even though it probably hasn't felt like it." She got a bit teary-eyed, and Danielle reached out to hug her.

When her mom pulled away to put the ground beef in the pan, Danielle said, "I'll take care of dinner, Mom. Just relax."

Her mother shook her head a bit, looking even more

shocked than before. "Did I just hear my daughter say she'd cook? I never thought I'd see the day when that happened."

Danielle feigned hurt and turned the cooktop on. "Well, I've been gone for a while, and I got sick of takeout after a while. Thanks to the internet, I've mastered a few recipes."

Her mother chuckled, settling onto a stool by the bar. "Word has it that you've been spending a lot of time with the bookstore owner."

Spinning to look at her mother, Danielle felt a wave of panic. "Whose word are we talking about?"

"Everyone from the book club. There have been a few others who've stopped me to ask what's going on between you two." The mischievous grin on her mom's face caused Danielle's stomach to sink.

Turning back to break up the hamburger meat, she asked, "What did you say?"

"I just said you had common interests, and since you were working on that article together, you'd been spending time together." There was a long pause before she said, "Or is there something else?"

Danielle sighed, twisting her neck to look back at her mother. "He asked me to dinner tomorrow."

"And?"

"We're friends. We can go to dinner, even though he'd like to think it's a date." She studied her mother's face and saw irritation flash across her eyes.

"Danielle, you need to stop putting up a wall. Liam's a good man, and the poor guy has been set up on so many dates here in town that I feel sorry for him. The fact that he asked you out is a big thing." Her mother stood and walked to Danielle, wrapping an arm around her shoulders. "Don't let what happened to me drive you away from love. If I hadn't married your father, I wouldn't have you. From the look on your face, I'd say you have feelings for him."

A rawness clawed at Danielle's throat as she mulled over her mother's words. "I don't want to get hurt, Mom, nor do I want to be the one to hurt anyone."

"What makes you think either of those would happen with Liam?" The earnestness in her expression made Danielle really think about it.

"I guess that's always been my perception of love. That there will always be some form of heartbreak, even if you stay together until you're old and gray. I just don't know if I'm strong enough to survive that." Danielle licked her lips, hoping to distract herself and hold back the tears like a dam.

Her mother pulled her in for a full hug, and they stood there for several seconds, the fear and sadness replaced by hope.

"It's okay to take things slow, but don't shut out the chance for a happily ever after too soon. Your father and I had some great times together, and even after the way things turned out, I wouldn't have changed it."

Danielle pulled back a few inches, her eyes searching her mother's. She'd never heard this much about her father, but despite all the heartbreak, Danielle was grateful her mother didn't regret the relationship.

Maybe love was worth taking the leap. Or maybe just one step at a time.

CHAPTER 20

*L*iam closed up the bookstore early the next day, wanting to make sure he'd prepared enough food for the event. As much as Danielle didn't want to call it a date, he did. There were so many nuances to her personality, and he wondered if he'd ever learn them all. She could be stubborn and sassy, while other times she could be empathetic and easy to talk to. Every time she saw Cari, she connected with the girl like she'd known Cari all six years of her life. Considering her out-of-the-box personality and his sister's words to find a girl in his head, he'd finally come around to the idea of wanting a future with someone.

With everything going well with Kara at the hospital and her last treatment, he'd arranged for Tasha to hang out at the house with Cari while he took Danielle on their date. Kara hadn't yet recovered completely from the previous surgery, and the doctors wanted to make sure they didn't send her home prematurely, even though her tests were starting to look more positive.

After loading a flexible bag with all the picnic items he'd

planned to bring, he searched around the kitchen, trying to remember if he needed anything else. A blanket.

Moving to the front room, he grabbed a large jean quilt Kara had made back when she and Cory first married. After throwing it next to the bag of food, he retrieved a jacket from the hall closet.

"Where are you going?" Cari asked, walking in from the other room.

"I'm going out with a girl. Tasha is going to stay with you for a few hours until we get back, okay?"

A wide grin crossed her face, and she did a fist pump. "I was hoping she would come."

Liam chuckled at her enthusiasm. He opened the front door with his arms loaded with the supplies and almost bumped into the teenager.

"Sorry, Tasha. Go on in. I'm just going to load this, and then I'll be in."

The girl smiled. "No problem, Mr. Pearson."

Liam scrunched his nose, feeling really old now that teens were starting to address him like that. After loading everything into his Jeep, he ran back inside. There were only a few minutes left before he was supposed to be at Danielle's house, and he didn't want to be late.

He found the two girls already playing with some of Cari's dolls. "Okay, I've got to head out now, but there's some money on the counter. You can order pizza for dinner, and feel free to play games, watch movies, or whatever you want to do tonight. I'm not sure what time I'll be back, but I'll let you know."

"Sounds good," Tasha said, turning back to Cari, who was already talking in an animated voice as the character of her doll.

Liam grinned. Feeling that push of excitement, his feet moved quicker down the stairs than normal, and he burst out the door. Settling into the driver's seat, he pulled out of the driveway and drove up a couple of streets to the Holloway home.

He'd done all he could to think of something fun for them to do, and as she'd grown up here, that made it even more difficult. Each place on his list had been considered more times than he'd wanted to count, but he'd finally decided on the Oakland Ranch. With several activities, like horseback riding, archery, and old cowboy games, it sounded like they'd be able to do something relaxed but fun.

Stepping onto Danielle's porch at four twenty-five, Liam took a couple of deep breaths, hoping to calm his racing heart even as he waited for someone to answer. Mrs. Holloway came to the door with a wide grin, an apron around her waist. The smell of fresh baked goods wafted toward him, causing his stomach to rumble.

"Good evening, Liam. I hear you're taking my daughter out for the evening."

"Yes, ma'am. I'll make sure to have her home at a decent hour."

Mrs. Holloway tipped her head back and laughed. "If it were ten years ago, I'd appreciate that. But Danielle's lived away from home long enough that I can trust her choices." She stepped back and let him in. "I wish you good luck and hope it goes well. She should be down in a minute, but you can wait in the family room."

Liam nodded, walking to the room she directed him to. "Thank you. How are you today?"

The woman nodded. "I'm doing quite well, thank you. I had a short shift at the grocery store this morning, and I've baked a few pans of muffins. Here, let me get some for you to take with you." She disappeared into the kitchen.

Liam smiled at her enthusiasm. She seemed to have a watered-down version of Danielle's personality, and he couldn't help but grin at the thought. Usually, it was the other way around with parents and children, but in the case of Danielle, she was bound to break expectations.

When Mrs. Holloway returned, she was holding a small white bag.

Peering inside, he saw several large muffins. "These smell really good. Blueberry?" Liam asked.

Mrs. Holloway nodded. "And a couple cranberry-lemon. If you don't eat them, take them home for you and Cari. I hope your sister is improving." She paused a moment, looking as though she shouldn't have said anything. "I'm sorry. Dottie McCready told me about your sister's diagnosis. Kara is such a wonderful woman. I was just heartbroken when I heard she was sick."

Liam dipped his head so she wouldn't see the visible force it took to swallow around the mound in his throat. "Thank you. We're hoping some of these treatments will help, and Cari is happy as long as she can see her mother every so often."

With a quick tap to his cheek, the older woman said, "I'm sure. Sometimes a girl just needs her mama, even when she won't admit it." She glanced up the stairs where Danielle probably was. "Even the stubborn, independent type need a support system to lean on." She winked at him.

He chuckled. Stubborn and independent were definitely words he'd use to describe Danielle Holloway. It was something he liked about her, her fierce spirit and zest for life. He'd dated a lot while in New York but always found girls who were looking for stability and security, meaning money. And that described Tawnee to a T, except that on top of all that, she wanted fame, doing everything she could to join every reality show out there.

While he had plenty of money saved up from his prestigious but stressful job in New York, he didn't want a girl to like him for his money. He wanted someone who would stick by him even if that money ran out, who would work with him to make it through those slim moments and come out stronger.

Footsteps padded along the hall above, and Liam glanced up to see Danielle walking down the stairs in a pair of jeans and a flowing yellow shirt. She looked like the sun, and Liam grinned.

"Sorry to keep you waiting," she said about halfway down.

Liam shook his head. "No problem. I was just talking to your mom."

Hitting the bottom stair, Danielle asked, her eyes wide, "What about?"

He didn't think she'd like being the focus of their discussion, and he glanced around, hoping to come up with something that wouldn't end the date before it began. Holding up the white sack, he grinned and said, "Muffins."

Danielle looked at her mother. "Did you convince her that she should start a business selling them? Her muffins are something I dream about when I'm not home."

Mrs. Holloway laughed, causing a chain reaction in the other two. "I'm sure you do. Well, don't stand around here all night. Get going, you two." She said it with a twinkle in her eye, and Liam was grateful. The woman was kind and gentle, and he could tell she loved having her daughter home, even for a short while.

"Thank you again, ma'am, for these. She's safe with me."

Danielle scoffed. "That remains to be seen. I can throw a mean right hook."

"If I ask you to bring a jacket, you won't hit me, will you?" Liam asked, one side of his mouth turning up. He'd have to watch his words around this one.

"Really? I think it was over sixty-five today." She turned and opened a door in the hall, pulling out a jacket.

Rolling his eyes, Liam said, "Can you just trust me for one night out?"

With another chuckle, Mrs. Holloway pushed the two of them out the door. Looking at Liam with a grin, she said, "Like I said, Good luck!"

The door closed with a soft click, and Danielle walked down the stairs. Turning, she looked back to where he still stood watching her. "Well, are we 'hanging out' or what?" The tug upward of her lips made him move, as if breaking a spell.

"Yep. We, uh, need to stop for a couple of drinks at the store because I forgot those." He lengthened his stride so he could beat her to the passenger side door, pulling it open for her.

She hesitated, like she wasn't sure what to think about that, before stepping inside. "Sounds good. I know the grocery store like the back of my hand."

As Danielle slipped into the passenger seat of Liam's Jeep, he couldn't help but grin, liking how she looked there. He hadn't realized how nice it was to be around another adult. Not that Cari was awful. She was one of the best kids Liam had ever met, but there was something about getting out and talking to other people.

The thought triggered a memory of his mother in the bookstore. With two young kids, that must have been why she talked to everyone she bumped into when he and Kara were growing up.

After putting her jacket in the back, he got in, turning on the ignition. The stop at the grocery store was quick, and Liam started driving toward the ranch.

"What do you have in mind for this evening?" Danielle asked, pulling several pieces of hair from her face that had blown out from the wind.

Turning to glance at her, Liam said, "It's a secret."

From Merkley's Grocery on Main, he drove north one block, making a right on Fourth Street. Heading past the fairgrounds, he turned left, driving back toward the mountain to the entrance of the Oakland Ranch.

"Looks like we're going really far," Danielle said with a laugh. "I'm picturing a dummy head stuck into a bale of hay and a couple of ropes."

At her comment, Liam laughed loud and deep, feeling more and more at ease with this girl. She kept worming her way past the first few walls he'd built after Tawnee's betrayal and the fear that he might lose another family member to cancer. He didn't think it would take much more for her to make it all the way to his heart.

"That's a great idea for another day. I planned something else." When he drove into Oakland Ranch, Danielle looked at him like he'd made a mistake.

"Why are we here?" A mixture of confusion and excitement spread over her face.

"We're going on a trail ride. Carter Oakland is lending us a couple of horses." He studied her face, trying to read the mask covering it.

"Points for creativity." She unbuckled her seat belt and slid out of the Jeep before he could make it around. He did his best to tell himself that she just needed some space.

They walked through the grounds and around to the stables, where he saw Carter had already saddled two brown horses.

Danielle got into the saddle with ease, surprising him again. She must have seen his expression because she gave him a close-lipped grin. "I was a pageant girl at one point in my life. Riding was everything for a while."

"Well, Miss Holloway, you never cease to amaze me."

CHAPTER 21

Danielle took the reins of the brown mare, feeling the animal move beneath her. It had been some time since she'd had the chance to ride a horse, but all the old knowledge seemed to flood back, telling her what to do next.

The horse was calm, and she was grateful for that. As much as she missed riding, she could still picture the last time she'd been on one. It was right after she'd been bucked off, and her trainer told her she had to get back on. Something about conquering fears right then. That was the last time she'd ridden, preferring to leave town for college, and she hadn't thought about it since.

Danielle hadn't noticed Liam pull a bag and a blanket out of the back of his Jeep, but he shifted it all to one arm and then handed her the jacket she'd pulled out when they left. Liam loaded everything into the saddlebags that were draped around the other horse and then mounted.

Carter Oakland directed them to the trail that led up into the mountain behind the ranch. The trees were a bright green, and the fresh mountain air filled her lungs. A pang of sadness hit her chest, and she realized how much she'd missed this. She'd thought life was best in the big cities with plenty to do—things to fill up her time so she couldn't think about all she didn't have in her life. But this was something she didn't know she needed.

"You look like you're about to cry. Are you all right?" Liam asked, pulling his horse up beside her.

"I'll be fine. It's just been a long time. I couldn't wait to get out of this town when I was in high school, and now…now I'm not sure what I feel." She looked out at the scenery around her, feeling like every bit of the crisp afternoon weather was seeping through to her soul. "It's been years since I've been up in this area. It's beautiful."

They rode in silence for some time, and Danielle was grateful for it, knowing she wouldn't be able to speak as she rode. Memories flooded through her, and that love of riding she'd had from so long ago was back, this time even stronger. There weren't many places she could do this in LA.

Glancing over, she saw him watching her every so often. She smiled. "What's new with the bookstore owner? Have you gotten any new mysteries in since yesterday?"

He shook his head and laughed. "No, I have this one customer who keeps coming in and buying them up." He gave her a pointed look.

She giggled. She hadn't felt this comfortable with a guy since high school, and those were all of her good friends, never a romantic interest. As much as she wanted to tell herself nothing was going on between her and Liam, her feelings for him were sliding out of control.

"How did the treatments go for Kara?" Danielle asked, maneuvering her horse around a large boulder in the path. She hadn't had a chance to ask, and she hoped the hospital would have updated him on her situation by then.

He was behind her now, and she had to twist to see his face, a sober look on it. "She's—Danielle, look out!"

She whipped her head back around to see that she'd been leading her horse closer to the edge than she thought, and the front hoof slipped on the edge a bit. She pulled the reins back, directing the horse along the path, her heart racing as she realized how close they'd come to tumbling down to the river below.

After another few yards, they were in a clearing. Danielle pulled the horse to a stop and slid down, still trying to catch her breath.

Liam did the same and stalked toward her, placing his hand on her back. "Are you okay? That was a good save."

Danielle stood straight up and was grateful his hand was still on her back, allowing her some support as she tried to keep the world from spinning. After several deep breaths, she gave him a quick smile. "I'm just glad you said something."

"Let's stop and eat here. We won't go much farther so we can make it back before dark." Liam unloaded the picnic basket and spread out a large blanket he'd stuffed into one of the saddlebags. As he laid everything out, she was impressed.

"You actually put thought into this. Thank you."

He opened his mouth, feigning hurt. "I take it your dates are more spontaneous than this?"

Danielle threw back her head and laughed. "That would mean I actually date. Thank you for all of this." She waved to the spread he was pulling out.

Liam handed one of the two turkey sandwiches to her, and she started unwrapping it from the large paper it was in.

"I'm just glad Troy knew your favorite sandwich." He winked at her, and she gave him a small smile, surprised that he would even think about what she would want. Then again, Troy Paul owned the sub shop in town and somehow managed to remember most of the townfolks' favorites.

"Troy does a good job of remembering that kind of thing,

even from years ago." She took a bite of the sandwich. "How did he know I like avocado now?"

"I'm not sure, but it was a good guess."

Liam pulled out a few small bags of chips and held them up for her to choose. She decided on one of the cheesy kind, and their fingers brushing sent zaps of electricity flying through her hand. The feeling faded as soon as he pulled away to open his chips, but her eyes lingered on his face, wondering if he'd felt the same thing.

After a few minutes of silence while they ate their food, Danielle turned to him. "Okay, I know almost nothing about you. Did you grow up riding horses?"

"Yeah, my dad was a vet, and I grew up in a small town in eastern Utah. Trail riding was something we did as often as possible. There were a few more people than here, but it still has that same feel."

"So, how does a guy from a small town end up with a job in New York?" Danielle asked. She took a bite of her sandwich and chewed as she waited for his answer.

Liam took a few seconds to swallow before answering. "I thought about moving to the city from the time I was thirteen or fourteen. Getting out of a place where everyone remembered every little thing I'd ever done wrong was a good motivator, and I figured that the big cities would be easy for anonymity. It was for a while, but a bunch of things happened, and I realized I missed the slower pace—and my sister and niece."

"I never would have pegged you for a guy who lived in New York. I like it there, although I'm not sure I could live there full time." Danielle thought about his answers thus far. It sounded oddly similar to her own life.

"You seem like someone who would love to live in Manhattan. I feel like that is the ultimate adventure: milling around all the people on the sidewalk and trying to drive anywhere during rush hour."

She tipped her head back and laughed. "I bet those are awful. I love to travel, and sometimes it's difficult to stay in one place for too long. I guess I inherited that trait from…"

When she didn't finish, he prompted, "Your father? Where is he?" From the pink tinging his cheeks, he looked like he regretted saying anything.

She smiled, hoping to help him feel at ease with the topic. While she'd held back a lot when it came to love, her mother had never outright bashed her father for the choice he made so long ago. That was probably why she didn't feel like she should hold a grudge.

"Honestly, I have no idea. I don't even have memories of him because he left when I was young. It's just been me and my mom ever since. There are things I do and wonder if it's just to prove something to my father. It's irrational, I know, since I don't know where he is."

"Do you wish you knew your father?" Liam asked, popping a chip into his mouth.

She paused. "I don't really know. I have days where I think of looking him up, and then others where I think he missed out."

Liam's eyebrows cinched together, and he reached forward, covering her hand with his. A warmth filled her, and she could only stare at their hands joined together.

"I just hope that when a situation arises, I'll choose differently than he did."

"You mean leaving?"

Danielle nodded, taking a swig of her fruit drink. "I understand feeling antsy about wanting to go somewhere, but if you have a family, that's the commitment you made. Work together to make plans to go places. Don't just take off and leave the rest of the ones you love just because you need to spread your wings."

"Is that you talking from an experience other than your dad? An ex-boyfriend who wronged you?"

Danielle's laugh was more exaggerated than usual. "No boyfriends, just a lot of one-time dates. And my job allows me an interesting perspective on people."

"Is that why you don't want to call this a date?" Liam asked, the corners of his mouth turning up.

"Maybe. Sometimes it just takes the pressure off if you don't refer to things as a date. Any ex-girlfriends in your closet?" She took the last bite of her sandwich and crumpled up the paper, throwing it softly at Liam. He picked it up and threw it back at her, causing her to giggle.

Liam laughed and then coughed, pounding on his chest. He took a drink of his sports drink and said, "I've dated."

She hesitated a moment, thinking he was going to continue. When he didn't, she said, "But that doesn't tell me anything. Was there someone special in New York?" She looked at him with her head tipped down, causing a smile to form.

"I dated a woman named Tawnee for about two years."

Danielle opened her bag of chips and popped one into her mouth. When she saw he wasn't going to continue, she said, "And?"

Liam laughed, tearing a few blades of grass and throwing them at her. "And she lied." His mouth closed, and she thought she was going to have to annoy him into telling, when he spoke again.

"I realize now how incompatible we were, but it took a lot to wake me up. I'd lost my parents and then Kara's husband, Cory. For a while, I just dated girls, making sure there were no real expectations. But then I was ready to settle down. Tawnee and I started dating, and things were great for a while, until she forged my signature for us to appear on a reality show."

Danielle paused with a chip almost to her lips. "Did they start filming?"

Liam nodded. "One of the producers came and said I'd forgotten to sign one of the release forms, and the story began to unravel. That was about eight months before I decided to move here."

Danielle had heard a lot of things, but going behind a boyfriend's back to sign papers for a reality show was a new one. Changing the subject, she said, "Favorite memory."

"I used to love when we'd go to a Colorado Rockies game as a family. We'd drive over once a year and buy peanuts and popcorn and hot dogs, usually sitting out in the outfield. I always brought my glove, and one time I actually caught a guy's homerun. I thought that was the greatest thing to ever happen."

"And what about now? Do you still have the ball?"

He nodded, his smile faltering a bit. "Yeah, I think it's in storage. I'll have to find a spot for it one day." He looked down, and something about his demeanor told her the subject was over for now. After several seconds, he looked up. "What about you? What's your favorite memory?"

Danielle scanned the trees surrounding them. She thought of the people in the town, of all the ones who'd helped her learn and grow through the years. But most of all, she thought of her mother.

"I don't really have one memory but a whole mashup of them. My mother is pretty much the most amazing person I've ever known. She's so selfless, and as I think about all the things she's ever done for me, I realize how much she's sacrificed, how much she wanted me to have a better life than she had."

"She's amazing, for sure. She's always asking how I'm doing."

Danielle took a sip of her drink. "I just wish I could do something to make her life easier. She won't let me pay her mortgage while I'm here, and I haven't had to do laundry yet when it's magically folded on my bed. She's a saint, and I feel so bad that I haven't always acknowledged that in her."

"Sacrifices are part of the territory when it comes to the people we love. Has she ever dated anyone since your father left?" Liam's eyes locked onto hers, and Danielle felt the same feeling she had when an airplane took off—that whoosh of something in her stomach.

Focusing on his question, she said, "No, I don't think she's really tried. My father broke her heart, leaving like he did, and I think it would be hard to move on from that. But she hasn't been catty about it. She's only told me the facts and left the emotion out of it, which was something for me to learn as a journalist. But I still have problems with that."

"Is that why you don't date anyone? You're worried about getting hurt?"

Danielle opened her mouth to say something, wanting to chastise him for being so blunt. As much as she wanted to deny it, her chest told her the truth. "I guess that could be one of the reasons. It's always hard to have a relationship as a journalist. I mean, I know people who do it, but when I'm sent to different states and parts of the world to write about things, it's easy for feelings to get hurt."

"What about now that you're here? Are you planning to look for another job like that?"

Liam's interest in her career left her wondering how he felt about her. Maybe he was trying to see if it was worth pursuing a relationship, and if that was the case, did she want that? She stared at the man again, seeing the kindness in his eyes, and the dimple in his chin wasn't half bad either.

Danielle shifted to lean back on her hand. "I'm not sure yet. There's a one-in-a-million chance I could get a job in that industry again, but I need to try. I'm not sure what else I can do with my time."

"Write your books?" Liam said with a grin. "You're so passionate about writing that I think you'd be great at it."

"You're funny," she said, a sarcastic tone coming through. She glanced up and saw the dark clouds above. "I don't want to cut this short, but we might need to head back. The rain up here can dump buckets, and then it would be a muddy mess on the way back down."

Liam nodded, kneeling and putting all the leftover food in the bag. Danielle bent down and grabbed the corners of the blanket, waiting for him to take the other side. As they worked together to clean up, she was transfixed by the softness of his features. They were only a few inches apart, and she thought about leaning forward to kiss him, wondering if he'd taste like the sour cream and cheddar chips he'd been eating.

A large clap of thunder sounded overhead, causing her to jump. The horses whinnied and moved, restless as they pulled against the reins around the tree.

Liam loaded the blanket and food quickly before untying both of the reins and handing Danielle's up to her after she mounted. She put on her jacket to protect against the rain, grateful Liam had thought ahead, and waited for him to slide on before starting the descent.

They'd made it about halfway down before large drops started to fall, but at this distance, she knew they'd missed the worst of it.

After another twenty minutes of riding, they pulled up to the ranch. The grounds were clear of people and animals, so Danielle steered her horse in the direction of the stables. Rain pounded on the tin roof overhead as they entered, and she could feel the horse shake a bit as it settled into the warmth of the shelter.

After dismounting, Liam pulled his horse into the stall next to hers and shut the gate. He fetched some oats from a bucket nearby and rubbed the front of the horse's nose, speaking softly to it, making Danielle's feelings for him soar.

She hadn't signed up for a relationship when she'd come home to Sage Creek, but she'd found a guy who was a good balance for her, one who she could rely on…if his feelings matched hers.

After his horse had eaten a fair amount of oats, Liam brought the bucket over to Danielle's and did the same.

Danielle leaned against the gate, watching as he worked. She'd never expected him to be like this with animals since everything she'd seen of him signaled an educated city boy. But this was just another side of Liam Pearson she'd unveiled, and it made her want to learn more.

Setting the bucket down in front of the horse, Liam turned, and Danielle was surprised at their proximity, the scent of his cologne making her dizzy. She looked up at him, saw his eyes watching her, and she was surprised by how much she wanted him to kiss her. The cold wet of her clothes clung to her body, and a chill swept through her, not all from the outside conditions.

He leaned down, their breath mingling together, right before the door swung open to the barn, sending the two of them jumping back. A silhouette came through the door, and Danielle couldn't tell who it was at first, only that she'd grabbed onto Liam's arm in the process.

"Did ya get caught in the rain?" Carter's voice came through, and after another few steps, his features were visible in the dimly-lit stable.

"Not too bad. Danielle suggested we head back, and I'm glad

we did." Liam looked down at her, his eyes warm and sending tingles throughout her body. "Thanks, Carter. I owe you one," he said, his hand resting gently on the small of Danielle's back.

He grabbed their picnic bag and blanket from the saddlebag and walked toward the door Carter had just come through. Danielle wished they were alone again, that they could recreate the mixture of tension and excitement she'd felt as he bent down to almost kiss her.

"No problem," Carter said as they passed him. "I'll hit you up when my wife is done reading all these books she just bought from you. I might have to have Colton come over and build me a library."

Danielle grinned. "I'm sure he'll be in the honeymoon stage for a while." The moment the words left her lips, she straightened and clapped a hand over her mouth. Why had she even said that?

The two men chuckled as they said goodbye. When they got to the door, Liam leaned over and whispered in her ear as the rain on the tin roof had only gotten louder. "We'd better run to the truck. Otherwise, we're going to get another shower."

Danielle nodded, and they took off, Liam grabbing her hand and linking their fingers together as they leaped over puddles on their way to where they'd left the Jeep. After she jumped inside, he shut the door quickly, hoping to avoid any more water entering. She flipped down the visor and looked in the mirror, wiping under her eyes and fixing the hair that had escaped the ponytail she'd had it in.

Liam laughed as he got in and started the engine, turning on the heater. The day had been hot, but with the cold water coming down, Danielle could feel the shivers coming on, and she was glad there was heat.

"I've got a dry blanket in the back. I'll go get it so you're warm." He moved to open the door, but Danielle stopped him with a hand on his arm.

"Just get it later. I don't want you to get sick from getting a blanket. The car will warm up soon, and we'll dry off."

Raising his eyebrows, he asked, "Are you sure?"

She grinned. "Yep."

Liam turned around and backed out of the spot, turning the wheel to the right to get to her house. Looking at the clock, it was only seven. As much as Danielle hated to go home this early, she wasn't ready for an all-day outing.

As they pulled up at her house, a knot twist inside her stomach, making her wonder what she should say or do. She didn't want to offend him by not asking him to hang out longer, but something kept holding her back.

"Thank you so much for taking me up there. I really needed it." She grinned.

He mimicked the gesture. "I'm glad. I wish it hadn't started raining." He undid his seat belt. "Here, I'll help you to the door."

Again, she caught his arm, her hand feeling the heat of his skin seeping through. "You're good. I'll just run in quickly. I'll see you tomorrow, maybe?" She heard the hope in her voice, and heat ran up to her cheeks.

"That would be fun. Thanks again for coming. I loved every minute." Their eyes locked for several seconds, the silence palpable in the Jeep. She thought he might lean in again, and the thought made her chicken out, breaking the spell of their gaze.

She opened the door and ran up the steps to the house, twisting the knob to the front door. After moving through and out of the rain, she poked her head back out and waved to him as he pulled out of the driveway. He smiled and nodded before his Jeep disappeared back down the road.

Danielle moved back into the kitchen, replaying the

moment in the barn of their near kiss. What was strange was how much she'd wanted it and how disappointed she was that Carter had interrupted them. Would she get another chance? Would he even want to?

All questions she couldn't answer right then.

CHAPTER 22

*L*iam walked into the house to the smell of pizza and popcorn. He heard a movie playing, probably the latest animated film that they'd watched at least ten times since Liam bought it for his niece. Peeking in, he saw Cari and Tasha sitting on the couch, both throwing kernels of popcorn in their mouths almost simultaneously.

"I'm back," he said, breaking their trance on the television.

"Already?" Cari whined. "It was just getting to the good part."

Trying to hold back a chuckle, he said, "Tasha can come back another time. Right now we need to get you ready for bed." He tipped his head down and looked out of the corner of his eye to say he was serious.

Cari frowned, crossing her arms in a dramatic fashion.

Tasha stood and said, "Thanks for playing with me, Cari. We'll have to find a way to get your uncle out of the house again, okay?" She winked at Cari, melting the little girl's mood away.

Cari made an O out of her hand and put it up to her mouth,

trying to make it so Liam couldn't hear. It might have worked had she not spoken in regular volume. "That would be awesome. Sometimes he just needs to talk to other adults." Cari used her other hand to point her thumb in Liam's direction, and he had to step back so he wouldn't burst out laughing.

When Tasha came around the corner, he handed her a few bills and opened the door for her. "Thanks again, Tasha. I really appreciate it."

"No problem, Mr. P. Thanks again for having me. Cari is a lot of fun." She waved and disappeared out the door.

Walking back into the family room, Liam whispered, "Who wants some hot chocolate?"

Cari stood, bouncing up and down with one hand waving in the air. "Me! I want some!"

Liam waved her over. "Run up and put on your pajamas. I'm going to change my clothes, and then I'll heat some up. We can finish watching this until bed." He pointed to the screen of the young heroine singing a song to the scenery and shook his head.

Cari ran out of the kitchen and up the stairs, her footsteps almost a cadence in his head.

He filled two mugs with water and placed one in the microwave, pressing the buttons to let it warm. He replayed the moment on the mountain where Danielle's horse almost slipped, and he shuddered, thinking of what could have happened.

But then his thoughts shifted to how close he'd been to kissing Danielle. For as much as she said she didn't want a relationship, he could feel the energy and could see that she wanted to kiss him too.

As the full impact hit him, he wondered if that would be good. There were still a lot of unknowns about his sister's case, and he wasn't sure if Danielle would be interested in a relationship that would have distractions while he was trying to help his sister and care for his niece.

But he'd be Cari's guardian if anything were to happen to Kara, and he was being selfish, not wanting to pop the new dream forming in his head of Danielle in his future. Cari was adorable, but he was biased, and he'd never had the opportunity to see Danielle interact with kids. Would she even want kids?

The microwave beeped, pulling him from those thoughts. That was way deeper than he needed to think for a first date.

Steps thundered down the stairs above him, and soon Cari appeared, wearing her flannel strawberry pajamas that were at least one size too small, the pant legs hitting above her ankle.

With a smirk, he said, "Those need to go into the too-small box."

"But we're drinking hot chocolate, and the rain is making it cold outside. I just wanted to wear these one more time before you hide them." Cari's eyes turned big, channeling her inner puppy dog.

"Fine. But I'll have to hide the whole box this time if you're going to keep pulling out everything you're too big for." He turned and emptied the packet of hot chocolate into her cup, stirring it around until everything was mixed. "Here you go, Princess Cari. Your hot chocolate, just how you like it."

Cari's nose wrinkled, and she gave him a sad look. "No mini marshmallows?"

Liam frowned. "Oh, I think we're out. I'll write it on the list of things to get when we go to the store. How does that sound?" He moved to the side of the fridge where he'd hung a piece of paper that already had cheese, seasoning salt, and hot sauce written on it. He tried not to laugh as he thought about how different his life had become now that he lived in

Sage Creek. He was making lists and running to the grocery store. His old self never would have believed it, having lived mostly on takeout.

"I guess I can survive. But when we get them, we have to have hot chocolate that night. Because I don't want to wait for you to go on another date." The serious look on her face was hard to resist.

Liam ruffled her hair. "I think we can arrange that. You think I need another date, huh?"

Cari beamed up at him. "That's the only time I get to play with Tasha."

They settled onto the couch with a blanket and turned on the movie again. As they watched, Cari's giggle cut through his thoughts now and again. He kept seeing Danielle, her long sandy-brown hair and her fiery personality making him grin even now.

At one point, Cari turned and asked, "How was your date?"

Startled, Liam looked at her, surprised she understood this much at such a young age. "It was good. It started to rain, which ended it early, but it was a lot of fun."

"Do you like her?"

"Yeah, she's really nice."

Cari's face turned mischievous. "No, do you *like her* like her?" She wiggled her eyebrows and ducked when Liam moved to swat the top of her head.

"Where did you learn about that?" He tried to keep from smiling, but the way she'd said it kept running through his mind. Were his feelings that obvious?

"Sarah in my class said she *like* likes Stephen. So, I kind of know what it means, but kind of don't." She looked at him expectantly, as if hoping he would clear it up for her.

Liam debated whether or not he should be the one to have this conversation with her and finally said, "You can like someone as a friend, or, as Sarah is saying it, she wants to be his girlfriend."

Cari's eyes opened wide, and one side of her nose turned up. "She wants to kiss him and stuff? That's gross."

Laughing loudly, Liam pulled her in for a hug. "Keep thinking that way, kid. Until you're older." He felt a poke in his side and looked down to see her finger jabbing into his rib.

"You're older. Does that mean Danielle is your girlfriend? And that you want to kiss her?"

"No, no. First, I'm not that old. And second, she's not— well, she's not my girlfriend. Let's just finish the show and head to bed. We'll have to call your mom tomorrow and see how she's doing."

They leaned back, and Cari snuggled up to his arm. He thought about their conversation and how Cari interpreted things with her six-year-old mind. Things were so clear-cut at that point in life. If only his own life could be that way.

CHAPTER 23

*D*anielle finished the first draft of book four that Friday, excited to get to the end but not excited to go through and make preliminary edits. When she'd sent Liam a text to celebrate, he'd volunteered to beta read it for her, but she wasn't comfortable with the manuscript just yet, nor was she ready for him to know she was MK Malone.

She checked the dashboard of her book sales, surprised to see the number of the other ebooks sold continuing to rise by the day. Were there really that many people in the world who wanted to download something she'd written?

Now that she was back in Sage Creek, she thought of the world as being only as big as the few thousand people who lived in the town. But remembering California, she knew this town was just a drop in the bucket in terms of the number of people out there.

Deciding she needed to stretch her legs, she went for a walk, her steps taking her through the upper streets of Sage Creek. It only took about fifteen minutes before she stood outside the bookstore, surprised that the lights were out so early on a Friday afternoon.

Where would he have gone at that time of day? She needed someone to celebrate in her victory of words, and he was the most likely candidate. He seemed to get what it took to be a writer, at least a small part of it, and now that she wanted to chat, he was nowhere to be found.

Thinking he might have gone to the diner, she walked in that direction, nodding to the occasional people sitting outside the shops. She opened the door to the diner and entered, searching the tops of the heads in the restaurant. With no luck, she walked to the counter and ordered a cherry chip milkshake, thinking she might as well celebrate on her own.

"Hi, Velda," she said to the owner, who was flying through the restaurant as usual.

"Ah, Danielle. How are things? Did Holly ring you up?" she asked, carrying a tray to the booth right behind her.

"Yep." She paused a moment before she asked, "Hey, has Liam been in here today?"

Velda set down all the plates and turned back to her. "Liam Pearson? No, I haven't seen him the past few days, actually. Which is odd. He usually brings Cari here for a meal at least once every couple of days."

Panic constricted her airway, and she leaned forward. He wouldn't have just left. With the bookstore and his sister and niece, it's not like he'd be running back to New York on a whim. Maybe Kara had a treatment he'd forgotten to mention.

She shook her head, realizing how attached she was getting to Liam. As much as it felt right, the thought scared her. What if he did decide to go back to his old life? Would he be like her father and just walk out?

Pushing those thoughts out of her mind, she tried to be rational. He'd set up a bookstore in town, and with his sister still getting treatments, he wouldn't just up and leave. His absence had to be because of his sister.

Danielle had given Becca a hard time about being scared of people leaving her life, but most of hers had left unintentionally, when her family died in a car crash on their way to her college graduation. There was so much more fear for Danielle, as the people she'd loved had walked out of her life. The connection she'd felt over the past weeks between her and Liam was getting stronger, and she thought about their near kiss almost constantly. The girl who'd promised herself she wouldn't get involved was falling hard and fast.

But did Liam feel the same?

Twisting her spoon in the ice cream, she took a large bite, doing her best to stop a brain freeze from forming. With the diner only sparsely populated at the moment, she pulled her phone out to scroll through posts.

Opening her email, she saw an email in her author inbox, the words *Liam Pearson* bolded. Her heart skipped a beat, and she saw that what she'd hoped wouldn't happen had, in fact, come to pass.

Touching the screen of her phone, she took a breath, hoping it wasn't what she knew it would be.

Dear MK Malone,

My name is Liam Pearson, and I own a bookstore in a small town in Colorado called Sage Creek. We have several fans who love your books, and I've had to reorder the first book at least three times in the last month.

I know it's a long shot, but we have authors come and speak as often as I can arrange, and if it's possible, I'd like to negotiate for you to come speak to the people of this town. The book group is full of avid fans, and we would make it worth your while.

Please let me know if that's possible so we can set something up. I appreciate your time and think you've done a great job with your characters, plot, pacing, etc.

Sincerely,

Liam Pearson

Danielle smiled at the simple and direct way he'd written the email, reminding her of the article they'd written. She'd only received a few emails from fans over the past few weeks, and they'd gone on and on about their favorite characters in the books, most of them not even mentioning the main character who solved the crimes. But not Liam. He'd requested it for the town.

She could picture him writing it, especially near the end where it seemed like he had just kept writing, unsure of how to finish the email. Had he taken several days to write it? Or was that just the quick thoughts coming out of his head?

She'd be an idiot not to give him a chance at a relationship, and yet, she wasn't sure how he'd take the fact that she'd pretended not to know MK Malone when they'd talked about it. She just hoped he'd forgive her when he found out.

But how would he find out? Should she reply back and say she couldn't make it? Or that she could—and have it be something like an exposé?

All the thoughts churned in her head and stomach, making her wonder if she should have eaten the ice cream at all. Why should she think he would even be interested in her for a real relationship anyway? She hadn't exactly been friendly to him in the beginning.

Blowing out a breath, she switched over to the messaging app, trying to come up with an excuse to text him that wouldn't be seen as clingy. They'd talked here and there since the date up the mountain, but he'd usually initiated the conversations.

Their article. Clyde had mentioned after the success of the first piece that he'd love to add their section to the paper at least once a month and, if possible, every other week.

When can you meet up to talk about the next His & Hers arti-

cle? I'm at the diner right now. We could chat tonight if you're available.

She stared at the screen until it dimmed and then turned to black, no message coming through. After paying for the milkshake, she walked out of the diner and down the road to the fountain in front of Town Hall. Taking a seat on the bench, she blew out a breath and tried to take her mind off it.

"Hey, Dani. I haven't seen you in a while. What are you up to today?"

Looking up, Danielle saw Susie standing in front of her. "Just trying to relax a minute before I get back to work."

With a somewhat genuine smile on her face, Susie asked, "Oh, what kind of work? I thought you weren't a journalist anymore."

Frowning, Danielle sat up straighter, and Susie took a seat next to her. "How do you know that?"

"I was in LA right before Becca's wedding and saw a few papers."

Danielle blinked several times, not sure what to say. "Did you tell everyone?"

The girl shook her head firmly, and Danielle sighed inwardly. "No, I wouldn't do that. I know how much your job meant to you, and if you were protesting against the city, you probably had a good reason for it."

Danielle searched Susie's face, surprised to see her smile genuine. Danielle had sent the evidence to the competing paper after getting fired but hadn't been checking the news enough lately to know what had come of it.

Reaching over, she patted Susie's hand. "Please don't say anything. I've only told my mom, Liam, and Becca, and that was tough as it was. It's just hard being seen as someone who had big dreams and then having those dreams crumble."

Susie pouted. "I get it. Don't worry. Mum's the word." She acted as though she were zipping her lips, even though a half-second later she was speaking again. "So, what were you working on?"

Danielle looked at her, trying to decide whether or not to tell her the full story. She hadn't even told Liam yet, and for some reason, she wanted to tell him before anyone else.

"I'm trying my hand at writing a fiction novel." She made her lips go wide with pretend shock.

Susie laughed. "I think you'd be great at it! I remember reading your stuff when you worked on the paper here and loving your wit and humor. I always wished I could be like that."

"But look at all the talents you have that I would be awful at. Figuring out how to decorate for bridezilla? Not my forte." Danielle had never had a heart-to-heart with this girl a few years her junior. She and Becca had always thought Susie a bit dim, but it seemed like she had a lot more depth to her than they originally thought.

Susie chuckled. "Honestly, I feel the same way sometimes. If I ever get married, I hope I have someone like you around to keep me grounded."

Danielle gave her a disbelieving look, her eyebrows cinched together. "Me? If anything, I caused more trouble for Becca's wedding."

"Yeah, but you were there. You helped get Becca's wishes to come through. I can only hope to have someone like that supporting me."

Danielle could see the panic in her eyes and scooted closer, pulling the taller girl next to her small frame in a side-hug. It was awkward, but Susie seemed grateful. From the little Danielle knew about her current situation, Susie's parents had moved to a bigger city long ago and rarely contacted or visited Susie in Sage Creek.

"Dreams come true, even if we have to change them a few times. If I'm here, I'll be your bridesmaid. Just don't make me wear tulle." Danielle gave her a close-lipped smile and leaned back against the bench, watching the water fall over the edges of each level on the fountain.

Susie smiled, wiping away a tear that was about to fall. "Thank you, Dani. I know we've never been close, but that means a lot coming from you. My advice to you is to go for it."

"Go for what?" Danielle asked, shifting her attention back to Susie.

"Liam. The way you two look at each other, it's like there's a magnetic field pulling you toward one another. I would've guessed you've known each other for a lifetime." Susie grinned.

Danielle turned back to the fountain, blinking. "We're not a couple, and we're not dating." It sounded so final, more final than she wanted it to be.

Susie stood, sliding the strap of her purse over one shoulder. "I didn't say anything. Just what I observed. I've got to head to the bakery. I'll see you around." She took a few steps and turned back around. "And Danielle? Thanks for the talk."

As she walked away, Danielle thought about her words. Should she go for Liam? But the whole thing about MK Malone was hanging over her head. He'd specifically said he'd broken up with his girlfriend because she'd lied. She wasn't committing any felonies by writing a book, but that might not be different in his eyes.

What was the best way to tell him both about being the author he'd emailed and attempt to tell him she might be developing feelings for him? Where was Becca when she needed her? A two-week honeymoon was far too long when so much was happening in Danielle's life. She was glad they'd finally be back later that day.

Ugh. She needed to keep her words to the page and hope she could just show him she liked him without crashing hard.

A text message sounded, and she pulled out her phone, smiling when she saw it was from Liam.

I'm so sorry. I had to head to Grand Junction for a bit, and I'm not sure when I'll be back. Pick a topic, and I'll work with it. I hope you're doing well, and I'll see you soon.

And like that, all the feelings she'd had for him were put in limbo. With such a vague text message, she wondered if she'd been imagining his feelings and intentions toward her. Was this just another friend-zone situation? She'd been friend-zoned a few times, and while it hadn't crushed every part of her, this general text could've been sent to anyone. She'd have thought that if he was about to kiss her, there would be more sentiment, more flirting.

Why didn't he tell her when he was leaving town? He'd see her soon? He'd been the one to initiate the date. Did that mean nothing? She wished he could have been more specific, but there she was, acting like some of the girls she'd always vowed to avoid. She didn't need to overanalyze it. The best way to play this was to act like she had when they'd first met, like he was just another guy in her path.

That's what she would do. She'd be nicer than the first time they'd met, but she wouldn't worry about dating him, let alone kissing him. It would work, and then she'd be back to the real Danielle Holloway, taking her dreams and bringing them to life. In a way.

CHAPTER 24

Liam had closed up the shop on Friday morning, knowing Kara would be getting her next treatment that day and wanting Cari to be there with her. They'd spent the weekend with his sister, and when the doctor said they were seeing some small improvements, his hope returned. They still weren't out of danger yet, but at least there was something positive to go with all of the heartache of it.

He'd gotten Danielle's text as he was driving, and part of him felt bad he couldn't hang out with her. But guilt soon followed, as he knew he needed to be there for his sister. He'd also missed the day with the guys, but Tanner and Colton understood. Liam just hoped Danielle would still want to get together when he came back home. Now wasn't the greatest time to start a relationship, but he'd figured out she was worth the juggling act.

Now, Monday morning, he was ready to start the week and get back to life at the bookstore. He'd just have to find a time to talk to Danielle, hoping she felt the same way he did.

"Are you ready to go to school?" Liam asked Cari as she sat eating her cereal.

"Already? I feel like I just woke up." Cari's eyes were heavily lidded, and Liam smirked. They'd stayed up a lot later than her normal bedtime the past few days, and he could understand why she was so tired.

"Yep, it's time to start walking over. Let's get your shoes on and grab your backpack." Liam pulled out the satchel he carried every day and waited by the door as Cari moved like molasses.

As he waited for her to get everything on, he pulled out his phone and checked his messages. When he opened his inbox, he was surprised to see a new email from MK Malone. Excitement poured through him, and he clicked on it with his thumb.

Dear Mr. Pearson,

Thank you for your email. It was nice to hear from a good fan. I've given it a lot of thought and checked my schedule. I'd be able to come to your small town next week if that works for you. Wednesday would work the best, so just let me know what time you'd like to have me arrive.

I will have a red flower on my lapel so you know who I am.

I'll wait to hear from you,

MK

"Yes!" Liam punched his hand into the air and laughed.

Cari scrunched her nose and stared at him. "Why are you so happy this early in the morning?"

Liam opened the door and walked down the front porch, pausing for Cari to follow. "I just got some good news."

His mind was in the clouds as they walked along, and he was surprised when they came to the corner near the elementary school.

"Hey, Liam. I was wondering if you were back or not."

Danielle's voice came to him like a song, and he turned, his cheeks hurting from smiling so wide for several minutes.

"We got back last night from the hospital." Should he tell her about the email he'd just received? Or would it be better as a surprise for her? It took him a minute to realize she was in workout clothes, a fitted tank top and yoga pants. "Did you take up running while I was gone?"

Danielle looked down at her clothes. "Um, no. That would mean the world is ending. Now that she's back from her honeymoon, Becca wanted me to try out the yoga class one of the ladies is putting on every week. I think they might bar me from entering ever again."

Her eyes moved down, and Cari stood up from inspecting a bug on the sidewalk.

"Hi, Danielle," Cari said, waving. "When are you going to go on a date with Uncle Liam again?"

Liam's body froze at her comment, searching Danielle's face for any reaction, good or bad.

"Well, I'm not sure. What if I want to come hang out with you instead?" Danielle knelt, looking at the young girl.

Cari grinned. "I can go for that."

Liam shook his head behind her. She'd been spending so much time with Tasha that she'd begun to talk like the teenager.

"I think we'll have to build a sandcastle or something sometime." Danielle stuck her hand out, and Cari took it, shaking it with a big motion.

"When? Can you meet after school gets out?" Cari swayed back and forth as she talked, and Danielle laughed through most of it.

Danielle glanced back up at him, and his heart skipped a beat, his mouth going dry as he awaited her answer. "I have something today, but maybe tomorrow? You should probably head into school, or you'll be late." The bell rang, and kids started entering the elementary school.

Cari gave Danielle a devilish smile. "He's free tonight, so you can go on a date." The girl laughed as she ran off in the direction of the front doors.

His mouth dropped open in shock. "Cari, hurry on to your class. I'll see you after."

Danielle's attention turned back to Liam, and he felt the shame of her stare. "How is Kara doing, really?"

"There are no major improvements yet. But she will be ready for surgery again in another week or two. If they can get everything out, she could go back to living a normal life. If not, she could go anywhere from weeks to a year before passing away." He locked his eyes with hers, seeing a betrayal there. He tried to think of what he could have done to give her that impression.

Her jaw tightened, and she rubbed her lips together as though trying to keep her emotions in check.

"I wish you would have told me. That you were heading out, I mean." She tucked a chunk of hair behind her ear and stared into his eyes, sending that tingly feeling flooding over him. Her words cracked at the end, and Liam felt like he'd been punched in the gut.

Reaching forward, he placed his hand on her upper arm. "I'm sorry. There's just a lot going on in my life right now, and when the doctors called and said we needed to hurry, I just took off."

Something about his comment changed her expression, like she'd been smacked.

"No, I get it. I just thought—" She paused, her expression looking like she was at war with some internal decision. "I just hope you're okay." She took a few backward steps away from him, heading in the direction of her street.

"Thank you for that." Her words opened hope inside him.

Someone cared about him, but not in a way to get ahead or lie about her feelings. "MK Malone agreed to come to the bookstore."

The sadness in her smile dampened his excitement. "Congrats, Liam. I hope it's a success." She turned and walked away, but Liam ran up and grabbed her arm.

"Danielle, I'm really sorry I didn't text you when we left. Can you forgive me for that?"

Her gaze went from his hand on her arm to his face, her lips trembling like she was about to cry. "You had to go. It was your sister. I should have figured it was something important."

They paused, staring at each other a few more moments before she said, "I'm sorry. I have to run. I told my mom I'd help her with some, uh, muffin baking." She gave him a small smile and waved as she walked down the street.

There was still something she hadn't told him, but maybe it would be better to let her tell him when she was ready.

CHAPTER 25

So many emotions coursed through Danielle that she was shaking by the time she made it home. After a long, hot shower, she felt a bit better, even though that seed of doubt had entered in.

Checking her email, she saw a response from Liam about MK Malone coming to the bookshop. Her stomach sank, a bitterness rising in her throat. How was she going to pull that off now? She'd sent the response on Saturday and had promptly forgotten about it. As she thought about the possessiveness she'd felt about him not telling her he was leaving, she felt guilty. But most of all, she was scared of how he would react when he found out she was MK Malone.

Sinking onto her bed, she stared at her dresser for several minutes, all of the scenarios passing through her head. There were only a few situations where he might be accepting of her deception so far, but she needed to come clean to him before the MK Malone appearance. She didn't want him to look like a fool in front of the entire town.

Pulling out her phone, she debated texting him an apology but knew it would be better to do it in person.

Will you meet me at the pizzeria tomorrow? I need to talk to you.

As if he'd been waiting for her text, his response came within a few seconds.

Of course. What time?

How about noon? Will that work with the bookstore schedule?

The response took a few more minutes this time before it finally came through.

Can we do eleven? I forgot I'm supposed to help in Cari's class after.

A smile played on her lips, and she nodded, even though she was alone in her room.

That works. Thank you.

PUTTING HER PHONE AWAY, she got up to dry her hair, hoping she'd be able to make it through her speech. She'd been so frustrated with him not contacting her, but he'd been taking care of his sister and niece, which she found endearing. But would he feel the same about her after she revealed she was MK Malone?

* * *

DANIELLE COULDN'T WAIT until eleven to speak to him. She'd been up half the night, tossing and turning over her decision to even say MK Malone would come to meet the town. She'd loved the anonymity and hearing what people really had to say about the books. And she'd liked getting to know the bookstore owner in the process.

Sitting on the bench outside the bookstore at eight, she pulled out her computer and started typing, trying to focus on the edits she needed to make in her book. But her mind was hyperaware of every sound around her, causing her to glance up every few seconds, hoping to see Liam's smiling face.

When she saw him strolling down the sidewalk from the elementary school, she turned her eyes back to the screen, wanting to at least appear like she was engrossed in the words.

"Hey, I thought we were meeting at eleven?" Liam said, laughing as he walked up to her. He slid next to her on the bench and met her gaze with his bright blue eyes.

"Well, I couldn't sleep last night, and I just wanted to talk to you first thing." She closed her laptop and slipped it into her bag. Turning to face him, she placed one hand on top of the other over her leg. After a deep breath, she said, "I just want to apologize for how I reacted yesterday. I shouldn't have done that. I guess it just hurt that I feel like we've gotten close and your sister being sick is a huge part of your life, but you didn't tell me about it."

"I know, and I'm sorry too. I can imagine you thought I'd taken off for somewhere." He winked and gave her a lazy smile, causing a giggle to bubble up in her throat.

"I also have one thing to confess to you," Danielle said, biting her bottom lip.

Liam raised an eyebrow. "Okay?" His voice was hesitant, and all of the things she'd pictured from the night before came rushing back. Was she ready to tell him the truth, only to have him back away from her like she'd done to him the day before?

Danielle opened her mouth to speak, but Liam's phone rang, and he looked down at the screen. He held up a finger and said, "The delivery truck is here with today's shipment, and I've got to get it unloaded or the guy will leave. Can we talk a little later?"

Frustration ebbed inside her chest, and she said, "This will take two minutes."

Liam stared at her, giving her his full attention. And with that, she chickened out. "I, uh, thought I had an idea for our next article, but I can't remember it anymore." Her explanation sounded lame to her own ears.

"Oh, okay. Well, I'll see you, maybe tomorrow? MK Malone is coming in the morning. I've got posters and flyers being printed right now. Are you going to come?" His gaze held her, and she nodded.

"Yeah, I'll be there."

Liam disappeared around the side of the building, and Danielle put her hands over her face, feeling the suspense as she knew tomorrow would be a total disaster.

CHAPTER 26

Liam woke early, unable to sleep because of what today would bring. He still couldn't believe MK Malone was actually coming to his bookstore. As he'd talked to a lot of people the night before while passing out flyers, he was surprised by all of the people who said they'd be there. He knew some of that was talk, but filling his bookstore with all the fans of MK Malone was more exciting than he imagined.

He'd been able to read the other two books in the series over the course of the past few weeks, when he hadn't been driving to Grand Junction or participating in some event in the small town. And when he'd received the email that the author was coming, he'd gone to the website and seen that there would soon be a fourth book, which he was sure the many readers in Sage Creek would look forward to.

He kept thinking about Danielle as well, hoping she'd come too. What was she trying to tell him with her expression?

He sent her a quick text. *Are you coming to the author event today? I hope to see you there today. Maybe we can get some dinner later?*

He dressed, checking his phone every minute or so to see if she'd responded. She was usually quick to answer back, but maybe she was sleeping. Shaking off the feeling of dread clouding his excitement for the day, he dressed and got everything ready for Cari to head to school.

Over the next two hours, he did as much research as he could on MK Malone and made a few dozen cookies out of prepackaged cookie dough. He was grateful that others had already volunteered to bring in other food items, but he hoped it would be enough for the crowd that would be forming.

He got Cari off to school a bit earlier than usual and worked in the bookstore, shifting furniture and trying to decide how things should be set up. Tanner arrived with a cartload of extra chairs they'd borrowed from the rec hall, and the two of them worked to get everything lined up, having all of them face away from the door to the back in the hopes that any stragglers would be able to find a seat without disturbing the crowd. Two long tables were set up on the far wall, and when the ladies brought food, it would be easy to direct them there.

People started milling around by ten thirty, chatting with neighbors and saving seats. The buzz in the room sent a rush of adrenaline through him. It was something he and Kara had always wanted, a chance for the community to come together to talk about books. He wished she was there with him.

At a quarter to eleven, there were only single seats sprinkled throughout the crowd, and Liam was pacing around the shelves, hoping the guest of honor wasn't standing them up. He'd worked with a few other authors for readings like this, but they'd always been early, leaving him time to talk to them a few minutes before introducing them to the crowd. Liam poked his head through the door and let his eyes search through the crowd, hoping to see someone unfamiliar with a red flower on his lapel.

The door to the bookstore opened, and Liam turned from behind the register, smiling when he saw Danielle walking through. She was dressed in a navy business suit, her hair half pulled back. The light amount of makeup she was wearing only accentuated her beautiful features, and he wished he didn't have to go into the next room right then. He wanted to feel like he had in the stable after their date.

"Hey! You made it. You look the part of a journalist today." He grinned at her as she joined him next to the counter and near the door to the adjoining room. She looked pained, trying to smile but it looking more like a grimace. "Did Clyde want you to write about this?"

"I need to tell you something." Her eyes focused on his chest and not his eyes, making the uncomfortable feeling from that morning return.

"Can it wait until after the reading? I'm still waiting for MK Malone to show up so I don't look like a fool in front of the entire town." He gave her a half-smile, but she didn't return the expression.

Moving her hand from behind her back, he saw a red flower in it. She stuck it into the lapel of her jacket. "That's what I need to talk to you about."

Liam's mind spun with the information, wondering if she was playing a joke on him. "I never told you that MK Malone said he'd be wearing a red flower. How did you know?"

Tears leaked out her eyes and onto her cheeks. "Because I'm MK Malone. I wrote those books, not thinking anyone would ever read them. When I got here, I was shocked that people were reading the books in their book group and discussing them around town. I've worked with my name plastered all over as a journalist, and I thought I loved it at first, but now that I know what it's like to not have my work connected to me, I didn't want to say it was me. I wanted to tell you, was going to tell you when I sent you the manuscript of my new book, but this all happened." She brushed at a tear as it rolled down her cheek.

"Why? We talked about writing several times, about you writing books. Why couldn't you have told me then?" Liam bit down, Tawnee's face flashing in his mind. Her lies of omission were what landed him on a reality TV show without his knowledge.

"I was afraid you'd look at me the way you're looking now, like you don't know who I am. I just wanted to spend more time with you, to see where it would go."

The same betrayal he'd felt from Tawnee seeped into him, making it difficult to breathe. He hated being lied to, especially if it was for selfish reasons on the part of the other person, as it made him feel like a fool. And he definitely was a fool for thinking he could trust again.

Taking in a breath, he nodded. "Okay, how are you going to convince everyone else you are MK Malone?"

"I'll do my best. But I've brought the manuscript for the next book I'm working on, and after I read a section of it, I'd like for you to go through it for me. Would you do that?" She looked at him with worry in her eyes.

"I'd have to think about that." Liam gave a curt nod and stepped toward the door. "I'll go introduce you now."

As he moved into the noisy room next door, Liam wondered what he was going to say now that he knew the real identity of the town's favorite author.

He raised his hand, and a wave of silence passed over everyone. Several hundred eyes stared back at him.

"Welcome, everyone. I know you're all anxious to get started with our guest of honor. I'm grateful to author MK

Malone for coming out today, and I'm going to let her introduce herself." Liam smiled and moved to the side, trying to keep himself from chuckling as the room erupted in loud whispers with several people questioning the gender of the author.

Several seconds passed before Danielle moved through the door. Instead of the group getting louder, it went quiet, barely a breath heard.

"Good morning to you all. I know you were expecting someone taller, probably male, but I am the author MK Malone."

"What is this? Did the real author not show up, so you're using a disgraced journalist to take his place?" Sharon Crestview said, a sneer on her face.

As angry as he was at the whole situation, Liam's defenses rose, and he stepped closer to Danielle. "That's enough, Mrs. Crestview. Please let her speak." He turned to nod at Danielle, and she gave him a grateful smile.

The group calmed down, the interest in the situation so thick that Liam was sure it could suffocate them after so long.

"Thank you for letting me speak today. I know it's a shock to most of you that I wrote these books, but it's true. Because of my journalism career, I decided the best way to release these stories was to use a pen name. Some of you know that I've been let go from my job in journalism in California, and now I'm even more grateful I have the pen name." Danielle clasped her hands so tightly that the knuckles were a bright white, sticking out more against the red of her hands.

"That still doesn't prove you wrote the books," said a male voice Liam couldn't place.

A few people started talking over each other, and Danielle

raised a hand and finally whistled, getting the speakers to settle down.

"MK stands for Mary-Kate, which is my mother's name. Malone is the name of one of the people I admire most from the news industry." She walked over to the door and retrieved a stack of papers, her confidence increasing with each step. Liam was curious as to what she'd planned, but he leaned back against the wall and waited for her to continue.

"This right here is the next book in the series, and I have brought it in the hopes that you'd let me read from it this morning." She raised it as if it were a glass she was toasting.

"I know you're a gifted writer, Danielle," Sharon said, her voice less snarky than her last comment, "but this still wouldn't help us know for sure that you are who you say you are."

Danielle opened her mouth to answer but was surprised when her mother walked through the door and said, "She is who she says she is. I've seen the accounts for where she uploads the books to the self-publishing platform."

Mrs. Holloway's comments sparked a fury, everyone talking so loud it was hard to hear anything.

After several seconds, the mayor stood and whistled again. "I know this sounds like a fabricated story, but Mary-Kate Holloway has always been as honest as they come. She wouldn't do anything to jeopardize this situation, and we should be celebrating that an up-and-coming author comes from roots in Sage Creek."

Danielle nodded in his direction, grateful for the people standing up for her.

"Go ahead and read us some of that book," Dottie McCready said, showing off a wide grin.

Danielle began reading, and like magic, the crowd was enthralled with her words, weaving the story through their heads. Liam smiled, knowing she had to be the author because of the similar tone of her words as in the previous books.

As he listened, he recognized a few of the same descriptions she'd used in other books. She was, in fact, the author, and while she had talent, she'd told him she had no idea who MK Malone was. But what did he expect? It wasn't like they'd declared anything official.

She finished, and the group got up and mingled, talking to her and each other about the news of it.

Liam had to retrieve a broom and dustpan to clean up crumbs one of the children had left from his cookie and was startled by a voice behind him.

"I'm really sorry, Liam. I meant to tell you yesterday." Danielle's voice was soft.

He glanced up at her, unsure what to say. "You have a real talent. I'm glad you finished the book." He motioned to the stack of papers in her hand.

Danielle turned her head, a smile playing on her lips. "But?"

"There are no buts. I think you're a great writer." He walked over to dump the contents of the dustpan into the garbage can.

"I didn't mean to lie to you. I just wasn't ready for people to know who I was. But I should have told you, because you've believed in me from the beginning." Her eyes searched his face, but Liam couldn't get past the betrayal.

He nodded, all emotion gone from his tone when he said, "Yes, I did." He turned walking to the back door and out.

Rubbing his hands over his face, he took in several breaths. Lying shouldn't be looked at as a serious crime, but for some reason, it felt like it was.

CHAPTER 27

After a day of celebration and hand cramps from signing so many books, Danielle couldn't shake the exhaustion of guilt she felt. It was like the look on his face was now imprinted in her brain, and every time she closed her eyes, she saw the disappointment and betrayal.

Grabbing her phone from the nightstand, she rolled over, still under the covers, and went through her morning routine of checking the news and her social media. As she clicked on her inbox, the screen changed and a phone call with an LA area code popped up. Swiping, she said, "Hello?"

"Danielle Holloway? Chester Sebring, chief editor from the *LA Sun*. It's come to my attention that you sent papers detailing the misdeeds of several government officials to our offices."

Danielle felt her heartbeat in her throat and finally registered that the man was asking for an answer. "I did, sir. I—"

"We have an opening as a news anchor in our prime time slot and would like to offer it to you. If you accept, we'd need you to come here by Monday to get started." Chester coughed, and Danielle barely registered the noise as she realized all of her journalist hopes hadn't been dashed.

"I appreciate the offer, sir. Have you investigated how far out the scandal went?" She was sitting up now, too anxious to stay still for too long.

She heard some papers ruffle, and then Chester's voice came over the line.

"Several people are to be indicted in the next few days, one of them being your ex-boss. None of us at the *LA Sun* have taken part in such despicable—"

"Do you mind if I think about this and get back to you?" Danielle asked, cutting off what was sure to be a long monologue on the virtues of the opposing newspaper.

"Certainly. Please let me know tomorrow morning so I can make arrangements to fill the position if you turn it down."

"Thank you, sir. I'll make sure to have a decision by then." Danielle said goodbye and then lay back down.

She'd wanted to have her job back for weeks, had wanted to get back out into the action of things, traveling all over and scooping the next big story. But something had changed, and she saw Liam's face in her mind, the way it had softened just before he leaned forward in the stables after their date.

But if he wasn't going to forgive her, she didn't need a full twenty-four hours to decide. Her decision was made. Now all she needed to do was tell her mother.

After sending Cari off to school, Liam arranged for Tasha to pick her up from school, and he drove to Grand Junction, needing to get out of town. The chance to check on his sister seemed like the perfect opportunity.

When he walked in, he saw the paleness of her face and heard the beeping of the machines. Her eyes were closed, her chest rising and falling rapidly.

He took a seat next to the bed, placing his head in his hands as he leaned forward on his knees. Sleep had evaded him the night before as he kept seeing Tawnee and Danielle, the two of them laughing at what he could only assume was him. But toward the end of the nightmare, Danielle's face would transform into the one she'd given him yesterday, with her brown doe eyes and her mouth pleading for him to understand.

"What's got you all tied up in knots?" a hoarse voice asked.

Liam looked up to see his sister with her eyes only open a slit and a broad grin giving her just a touch of color to her cheeks. He forced a smile and leaned back in the chair. "I just needed to get out of town."

Her mouth dipped into a frown with his response, and Liam turned his gaze to the wall. "Liam, you can't push her away."

Frustration rose in his chest and up his throat. "She lied to me, Kara. Not just a little white lie, either. It was a big one."

"It couldn't have been worse than Tawnee's." Her pursed lips and raised brows reminded him of getting a lecture from his mother years ago. "Finding out you're on film for a future reality show is what I'd consider a big one."

"She's the author of those cozy mysteries everyone in town has been reading, MK Malone. We talked about the author and how Danielle could do something similar so she could stay in Sage Creek. The whole time it was her."

A weak chuckle came from Kara, and Liam worked to keep the irritation at bay. "If that's the worst she's done, I'd say you're okay, Liam. Think about it. She's been on billboards and has traveled all over the world for her career. Writing might have been her one thing she could do without receiving a ton of criticism."

Biting the side of his lip, Liam tried to think of it from that perspective. It wasn't like Danielle had been working to be seen through her books. And it seemed like she hadn't told anyone but her mother. For a woman he'd seen as adventurous who couldn't be tamed, it almost seemed like she now needed the stability she hadn't had since leaving Sage Creek.

Being humiliated in front of people he didn't know just in Manhattan had been eye-opening for Liam. He'd only been part of the pilot episode when he found out they weren't just doing it for some contest Tawnee had won. He couldn't imagine being let go from his career and then having someone he cared about distancing herself after he'd been afraid of a similar criticism. And yet that's exactly what he'd done.

Kara reached out, her fingers cold on his forearm. "Go talk to her. From everything I've heard, I think she's the one for you."

"Who have you heard things from?" Liam asked, crossing his arms and tipping his chin up in curiosity.

"My daughter sees all, dear brother." She smiled and laughed a bit, which turned into a cough.

Shaking his head, Liam couldn't help but laugh. "She takes after her mother." He paused a moment and stood. "How are you?"

"I'm good. Now go! Don't let her get away." She made a slow sweeping motion with her arm, and it looked like she'd used all the energy she had to do it. "Just make sure to bring her here once you tell her how you feel."

"Deal." Liam leaned down and kissed her on the forehead. Leave it to Kara to help him work through his problems when she was lying on a hospital bed.

* * *

LIAM HAD ORDERED a half-dozen muffins from Mrs. Holloway on his way back, claiming he needed them for a bookstore event. He hoped he'd catch Danielle at home, and from there, at least ten scenarios went through his head.

The door opened, and Mrs. Holloway greeted him. "Liam, it's so good to see you this afternoon. Come in, and I'll get your muffins packaged up."

Liam followed her into the kitchen and glanced around, seeing the rows and rows of muffins. "You made all of these?" From the looks of them, there were several different kinds, all waiting on the counter. Along with flavors, there were three varying sizes: mini, regular, and large.

Mrs. Holloway laughed. "Oh, well, I love to bake. The people of this town seem to like them as well." She handed him a yellowish one with several small black dots, likely lemon poppyseed.

Liam took a bite and grinned. "That is the best muffin I've ever tasted. You should really open up your own business selling these."

She frowned. "How can I do that when I've been giving them away for so long?"

"Believe me. People will pay for this." Liam pointed to the muffin and stuffed the rest of it into his mouth. After he'd chewed and swallowed, he looked around, trying to hear any other sounds in the house. Finally, he asked, "Is Danielle here? I was hoping to talk to her."

Mrs. Holloway grimaced and shook her head. "She left for California about thirty minutes ago with her suitcase packed. I guess the opposing news channel offered her a job after she'd let one of their staff know about the water dumpings."

Liam felt like he'd been kicked in the gut several times, wanting to double over from the information. "Did she say anything about yesterday?"

She turned away, but Liam saw the disappointment on her face. "Just that maybe she wasn't meant to stay in Sage Creek much longer."

Something about that didn't add up. "What do you mean, 'Wasn't meant to stay longer'?"

The woman turned around slowly, as if she was hiding something. "She's running."

"From what? From me?" Liam's voice broke on the last word.

She nodded and swiped with her pointer finger underneath her eye. "I think she loves you, Liam, but she's scared. Scared that you won't think she's enough. I've tried to help her over the loss of her father and explain that it wasn't her fault he left, that he just needed something different. I think that's been a driving factor in her life until now."

Liam licked his lips, feeling the moisture in his mouth disappear. His anxiety was skyrocketing, and he wasn't sure he'd be able to catch her before it was too late. If she made it to California before he could speak to her, she might close her heart off completely. "Where can I find her?"

Mrs. Holloway grabbed a piece of paper and scribbled something on it before handing it over to Liam. "That's the address to her apartment. If she's not there, she'll be at Channel 5 News in LA."

He wrapped his arms around the woman and hugged her. "Thank you."

His insides feeling like he was going up and down on a rollercoaster, he jumped in his Jeep. This was going to be the longest drive of his life.

"What are you doing in here so early, darlin'," Velda asked, pushing a strawberry milkshake over to Danielle.

Taking a large scoop, Danielle let the ice cream melt in her mouth, savoring the flavors before answering. "Just trying to decide if I'm making a big mistake or not."

The older woman leaned forward on the counter, her eyes open a bit wider, signaling she was willing to listen. It was just after noon, and there were several booths occupied, but the woman must have sensed Danielle needed someone to talk to.

"I got a job offer from an opposing news station back in LA." She took another bite. Folding her arms on the counter, she rested her chin on top, staring at the glass cup.

"And? Are you taking it?"

"I was going to. I have my suitcase packed and the car all gassed up. But something just doesn't feel right, like I'm missing something."

Velda's face broke into a wide grin. "Or someone." She

stood and put her hand on her hip, exuding the attitude Danielle loved.

Nodding, Danielle said, "Yeah, but that someone doesn't trust me anymore. I lied to him, Velda. Lied to him even after he told me he couldn't stand liars."

"Was it the book-writing thing?"

"Yes. I wasn't ready to tell anyone, not until I agreed to the author visit. I'd already burned one career, and I was worried I'd ruin this one if I told anyone. And now I've lost the man I think I'm in love with." Tears streamed down her cheeks, and she did all she could to keep from sobbing, knowing she was already getting stares from the people around the counter.

"If a man won't forgive you for one sincere lie, then he probably isn't worth your time," a male voice said from behind her.

Turning slowly, Danielle was surprised to find Liam standing there. As she studied his face, she couldn't get a good read on his emotions, but the words rotated in her mind at high speeds.

"What if he's been hurt before?" she said, trying to keep the emotion out of her voice.

Liam took a few steps toward her, his hands reaching for hers and sending that shock wave of electricity through them. "He should have realized the girl of his dreams wasn't the one who'd caused those trust issues."

His blue eyes looked back and forth into hers, and he leaned forward, wrapping his arms around her. She returned the hug, feeling the dam break on the emotions she'd been holding back.

"How did you find me here?" she managed between sobs.

"It's a small town. There were only so many places to look." He brushed the hair back from her face gently. "And I might have seen your car outside."

Danielle laughed, wiping at the tears.

His lips came next to her ear, and he whispered, "I'm so sorry. With all the success you've had with your books, I should've been the first one to be excited that it was you who wrote them."

Danielle wiggled her head against his shoulder. "I should have told you beforehand, when I realized how much you meant to me. But when you told me about being betrayed by your ex-girlfriend, it made it hard for me to want to say anything."

Liam leaned back, taking her head between his hands softly. "I love you, Danielle Holloway, for being just who you are."

"I love you too," Danielle said, a lone tear sliding down her face.

She never thought she'd be able to say that to anyone or that she'd even want to. But as she reflected on the words, she realized that every scrap of loneliness she'd felt before was gone.

Leaning down, Liam brushed his lips across hers, setting her nerves on fire. She wrapped her arms around his neck, pulling him in for a more intense, passionate kiss.

Clapping began around the diner, and she pulled back, rubbing her lips together as the sensations continued to fire in her nerves. She looked at Liam and grinned as they put their foreheads together.

"Just promise you won't leave me," Liam said, his voice barely a whisper.

"As long as you won't leave me."

He licked his lips, his gaze more intense than she'd ever seen it. "If something were to happen to, uh, to Kara, I would be the guardian of Cari. We're kind of a package deal."

Danielle pulled him in for another kiss, his lips soft

against hers. When she pulled back, she said, "You wouldn't be the man I love if you didn't take care of family."

He gave her a peck to the lips and said, "You were really going to take that job?"

Danielle laughed, all the pieces connecting now. "I discovered there are a lot of things here for me, and even though I thought about taking that job for a few seconds, I realized I'd be making a bigger mistake by leaving than by staying."

With a half-smile on his face, Liam asked, "What kind of things would you be missing out on if you left?" His arms wrapped around her middle, pulling her closer.

Danielle tried to keep her face neutral, but the corners of her mouth twitched. "That would be you."

EPILOGUE

After stopping for boxes at a store around the corner from her apartment, Danielle got to work packing up all she owned in LA. With the edits and marketing of her fourth book, as well as slowly convincing her mother to set up a muffin shop in the bookstore, she hadn't had time to come back and get everything cleared out. The lease was up at the end of the month, and she and Liam had made the decision to get it done that weekend before another storm was due to hit Sage Creek.

She worked late into the night, leaving some of it for the next day. As she worked, she thought of Liam and her new life in Sage Creek. Had anyone told her four months ago that she'd be moving back to her hometown, she'd have laughed in their faces. But Sage Creek felt more like home now than ever, and she hoped to make it so for the future.

Finishing up the last few things by close to four the next afternoon, she looked out the window and saw Liam pull up with the moving truck outside. Meeting him downstairs, she kissed him good and long.

"Thanks for coming to help me with this," she said, wrapping one arm around his waist as they walked back inside.

"Of course. What are boyfriends for?" Liam grinned, and they moved up the stairs together.

It had been three months since she'd turned down the network job, and with Kara's treatments, this was the first time they'd been able to get away long enough to pack up her apartment in Los Angeles.

Danielle loved Kara, who'd become the sister she'd never had. Her body had been reacting well to the course of treatments, allowing her to come home from the hospital for a few weeks at a time. The doctors were skeptical that it would last for long, but Liam and Danielle were determined to make the best of the time she had left, with that sliver of possibility that she'd survive for more years to come.

They worked throughout the afternoon, up and down the stairs with several boxes and the few pieces of furniture from the apartment. The weather was perfect for January, and Danielle was grateful for the lack of heat.

"Let's get something to eat before we head out. Is there somewhere you've been dying to eat or just want to have one last time?" Liam asked, inserting the keys into the ignition of the Jeep. They would leave the moving truck by the apartment until after dinner and then would head out from there.

Danielle pulled up a mental map of the area, trying to decide where to eat. "There is this Italian place a few blocks over I've always wanted to try. Just never took the time to do it."

She directed Liam to where it was, and the hostess got them right in. The woman smiled at them on the way back to their table, making Danielle feel a bit uncomfortable.

"Here is your table and your menus. I'll send your waiter out now."

"That was odd," Danielle said, scanning the options for entrees on the menu.

Liam shifted uncomfortably but didn't say anything, his eyes focused on the options as well.

They ordered their food, and for the first time since that day when they'd decided to be a couple at the diner, Danielle felt some weird invisible wall between them.

"Are you all right?" she asked, reaching out for his hand.

"Yeah, I'll be fine."

Danielle tried to study his face, even hoping to catch his eye so she could understand why he was acting so oddly after a day of laughing and chatting as they packed up the apartment.

"Did I do something wrong?"

Taking in a deep breath, Liam looked up, giving her a hesitant smile. "There's something I've been wanting to ask you, and I wasn't sure how to do it." He dug into the pocket of his jeans and pulled out a small silver ring with a teardrop pearl set in the middle. Sliding out of his seat, he knelt on the ground, looking at her with tears forming in his eyes.

Danielle took in a breath, not really believing this event was happening.

"Danielle Kate Holloway, since the day I met you at my bookstore, I've grown to love you more than I ever thought possible. Will you be my wife?"

Dropping down to kneel by him, she wrapped her arms around his neck, her tears already falling onto his neck and shoulder.

"Yes. A million times, yes."

Thank you for reading *Love, Under Review!* If you enjoyed it, I would love to see a review from you. You can also subscribe to Britney's newsletter here:

Subscribe to Britney's List

www.ingramcontent.com/pod-product-compliance
Lightning Source LLC
Chambersburg PA
CBHW021334190726
48288CB00003B/1107